# Dueling with the Three Musketeers

# the Enchanted Attic

**BOOK THREE**

## Dueling with the Three Musketeers

L.L. SAMSON

ZONDER**kidz**

ZONDERVAN.com/
AUTHOR**TRACKER**
*follow your favorite authors*

ZONDERKIDZ

*Dueling with the Three Musketeers*
Copyright © 2013 by L. L. Samson

This title is also available as a Zondervan ebook.
Visit www.zondervan.com/ebooks

Requests for information should be addressed to:
Zonderkidz, 5300 Patterson Ave., S.E., Grand Rapids, Michigan 49530

Library of Congress Cataloging-in-Publication Data

Samson, L. L., 1964-
    Dueling with the three musketeers / L.L. Samson.
       p. cm. – (The enchanted attic)
    Summary: Twins Linus and Ophelia and their friend, Walter, hope to rescue
their friend's school from the headmistress' greedy brother with help from
D'Artagnan of The Three Musketeers, but their plans go horribly awry.
    ISBN 978-0-310-72799-6
    [1. Space and time—Fiction. 2. Characters in literature—Fiction. 3. Dumas,
Alexandre, 1802-1870. Trois mousquetaires—Fiction. 4. Books and reading—Fiction.
5. Brothers and sisters—Fiction. 6. Twins—Fiction. 7. Orphans—Fiction.] I. Title.
PZ7.S1696Due 2013
[Fic—dc23

2012029258

The author is represented by MacGregor Literary, Inc. of Hillsboro, OR.

Zonderkidz is a trademark of Zondervan.

*Cover design: Kris Nelson*
*Interior design: Ben Fetterley*

*Printed in the United States of America*

13 14 15 16 17 /DCI/ 27 26 25 24 23 22 21 20 19 18 17 16 15 14 13 12 11 10 9 8 7 6 5 4 3 2 1

For Gwynnie

# Contents

# one

# As If It Wasn't Hot Enough

## *or* Let's Set Up the Major Conflict Right Away, We'd Hate to Bore You From the Beginning

𝒜s twins Linus and Ophelia Easterday slept, the desolate, most middle-of-the-night hour of 4:00 a.m. was not the only thing approaching Rickshaw Street where they lived above a bookstore with their aunt and uncle, Portia and Augustus Sandwich. Oh, the bookstore! A stone face with bay windows on either side of the door, ivy cascading down from its walls, promised all manner of wonderful reading inside it.

The twins had no idea a figure dressed completely in black silently swung open the black iron garden gate of The Pierce School for Young People next door. The thin, skulking intruder must have been at least six feet five inches tall and didn't seem to mind that fact at all. He wore his height without shame, his spine straight and stiff. A messenger bag hung from one shoulder and his steps were measured and precise.

But Linus and Ophelia weren't awake, so when their good friend Walter came bursting through the secret door in the bathroom that hid a secret passage between the school and Seven Hills Rare and Better Books, they didn't hear him either.

He ran into Linus's bedroom and pulled down the sheets on his friend's bed. Linus, six feet one inch tall, sat up automatically. "What?!" he cried, raking both sides of his bright blond hair, his blue eyes the size of lemons.

"Hurry, mate!" Walter yelled, pulling his friend out of his bed. "Someone's set fire to the school!"

"Where's Clarice?" Linus asked about his girlfriend as he was being yanked into the hallway.

"She decided to spend the night at her grandmother's house."

Ophelia opened the door to her room. "Did I just hear correctly?" She rubbed the corner of her right eye with her index finger. A disgusting glop had settled there, which just goes to show you, even in slumber no one is completely safe from slimy substances. Even our own bodies betray us! Egads!

"Yes!" cried Walter.

"Did you call 9-1-1?" she asked.

Walter shook his head. "What's that?"

He isn't a dullard. He's just from London.

"9-9-9," said Linus.

Ophelia shot a look at her brother that basically said, *How did you know that and I didn't?* "I'll call. Do not go over there you guys! It's dangerous."

"Right," said Walter.

She hurried down the steps to the kitchen.

"Madge okay?" asked Linus.

Walter assumed a look of horror. "I didn't think—"

"Let's go." Linus hurried toward the bathroom.

Walter followed, they both knelt on the green tile floor and disappeared into the open square next to the bathtub.

By the time the boys emerged in the cleaning closet on

the second floor of the school in the boys' dormitory wing, the sirens of fire trucks could be heard coming down the street.

Linus breathed a sigh of relief. If throwing a bucket of water on a little blaze in a trashcan was necessary, well, fine. But he did not relish the thought of becoming a human torch for the sake of a school he couldn't afford, or Madrigal Pierce, (whom they *lovingly* referred to as Madge) the headmistress, who constantly snubbed his family.

Walter, however, was on a mission led by his nose. "It's down the stairs. Let's go!" He placed his bottom on the mahogany handrail and slid down in an instant. Linus followed suit. He always liked this place. Imagine a cheerful, clean haunted house and you might get a clear mental picture of The Pierce School for Young People.

Black smoke snaked out from the back of the house, the private quarters of Madrigal Pierce, not only the headmistress, but owner, fundraiser, math teacher, purchaser, and Jill-of-all trades as well.

"I didn't realize it was coming from Madge's quarters!" Walter ran through the formal entry hall and back to the hallway leading to the prim woman who made herself the nemesis of everyone she came in contact with. "Breathe deep, mate!"

Linus did.

"Close your eyes!" Walter pushed open the door and smoke hit their faces.

They dropped to their knees and crawled toward Madrigal's bed.

*A word of instruction here, dear readers. Listen to the fire marshal when he comes and gives a talk at your school. He has good things to say and you might end up saving a life, someone else's or your own. Whatever you do, don't go back in for your computer. Trust me, a fresh start is never a bad thing, and generally speaking, it's better than death.*

The headmistress had already passed out from inhaling the smoke that was billowing in from the bathroom.

They pulled her off the bed. Linus grabbed her wrists, Walter her ankles, and, bent double, they slung her from the room and into the main hall. Linus was about to open the door when the firemen kicked their way through.

"At the back!" shouted Walter, then proceeded into a coughing fit.

Men in tan suits with bright yellow reflector striping trampled through with a hose.

Linus, coming out of his coughing fit, leaned down and placed his ear by Madrigal's mouth. "Breathing. Shallow."

"Good."

Not thirty seconds later, two paramedics relieved them of their post at Ms. Pierce's side.

As they worked to bring her back to consciousness, one of them looked up. "You might have saved her life."

The boys nodded and watched as the paramedics got Madrigal into a major coughing fit. Neither could bear to see the proud headmistress in such a state. They left the room.

"She'll be okay," said Linus.

Walter couldn't help himself. "I don't know whether to laugh or cry at that."

They sat at the bottom of the grand staircase in the entry-way, answering questions, wishing they knew more, watching a now conscious Ms. Pierce staunchly refuse to go to the hospital.

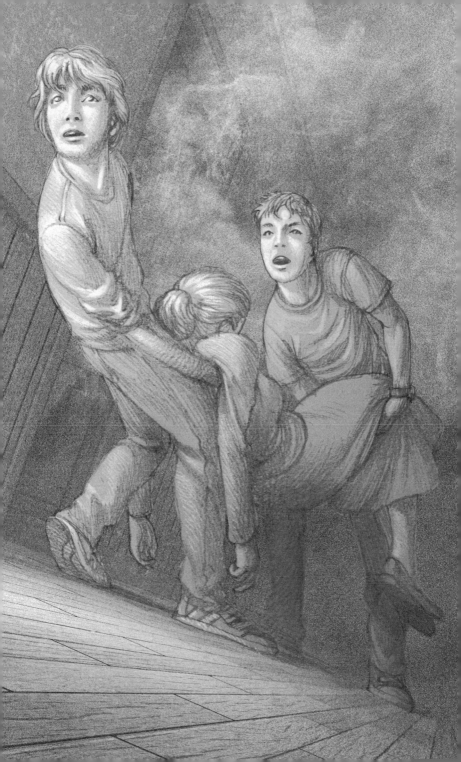

"Let's check on Ophelia," said Linus, and they went up the steps.

They crawled through the passage, only to be met in the bathroom by a rather furious Ophelia who stamped her foot, her dark curls bouncing in time, and pointed at each boy. "You deserved more than looking like chimney sweeps. I was so worried. I'm furious!"

They both shrugged. After all, a lad's got to do what a lad's got to do.

"Now look at yourself in the mirror and get cleaned up."

She turned and left the room.

"She'll get over it," Linus said. He was used to her bossy ways.

Walter and Linus caught their reflection in the mirror over the sink. Black, sooty faces stared back. Linus's light blue eyes contrasted with his skin like a patch of sky surrounded by storm clouds. Walter's warm brown eyes glowed like amber.

*Not that they would have described themselves like that. Heaven's no! Ophelia told me all about it. She visits me in the English department here at Kingscross University, and, between you and me, she's still mad they went into that house "with no thought for anybody other than themselves."*

*We've all learned not to mention they were trying to save lives if need be. Oh no! She'll have none of that.*

"Good thing Clarice wasn't there," said Walter, turning on the sink faucet.

"Definitely," said Linus.

*By the way, Clarice and Linus are official. What that means to fourteen-year-olds I cannot say, for I haven't an idea, nor do I wish to. Furthermore, I don't think I ever will.*

## two

# You Can Put Lipstick on a Pig, but It's Still a Pig

### or Backstory in One Place Isn't Always Good, but at Least This Backstory Is Interesting

(Backstory: What happened before the book began so you can better understand what's going on in the pages at hand.)

Oh dear, it had to happen in the most dreadful season, the dog days of summer, as people for years have been calling heat over one hundred degrees lasting for seemingly weeks on end. *"The dog days of summer" is a cliché—an overused expression that practically everyone has heard and uses in everyday speech, which is fine, but it's a no-no for writers—however, I say, if the shoe fits, wear it! (That just never stops being humorous. Oh, you think it does? Well, I'll forgive you.)*

The month of August entered the town of Kingscross with a vendetta against dry armpits. It sought to drain as much perspiration from as many people as possible. Paris Park's playground only held children in the early hours of the morning or in the slightly lessened heat of the evening. The public pool enjoyed more popularity than ever but only with people who didn't have air-conditioning. And the sales of popsicles went up 248 percent according to the *Kingscross Daily Herald. How they knew, I cannot say, so don't ask.* Folks everywhere were losing their tans due to the desire to stay inside, sit by the air-conditioning vent, and watch cable television. *Hopefully, they forewent those ghastly reality television shows that try to pass for entertainment these days. I'd hate to think of all that gray matter (brain tissue) dying off like good music.*

Of course, Uncle Augustus was too miserly—cheap, parsimonious, or just plain tight with his money—to actually install air-conditioning in the living spaces above the bookstore. Therefore, his great niece and nephew, Ophelia and Linus, left in the care of Augustus and his twin sister Portia, had become the laziest pair of human beings ever to live in the town limits of Kingscross. They lazed about in the leather chairs in the bookshop reading and reading and reading and eating red licorice sticks. Ophelia loved good stories; Linus enjoyed books about scientific things.

Linus kept a handkerchief on the arm of his chair to wipe his mouth after coughing up soot every so often.

The twins' parents had it no better at that time, and I for one smiled at the thought, further cementing my opinion that there is justice to the workings of the universe. *You see, the Drs. Easterday, scientists working on their butterfly project on some remote tropical island called Stu, were bowed under by an oppressive heat that made Kingscross feel like Alaska by comparison. They deserve it, the rotters! Imagine your parents leaving you for five years, five years, to study insects. That will give any child a basic inferiority complex—the mistaken belief that one is a lesser human being than others.*

Thankfully, the twins had each other, and if you guessed

their parents didn't really pay all that much attention to them anyway, you guessed correctly. They had always relied on each other, those two, and they still did that sweaty afternoon where one felt sorry for animals because of all that fur. Furthermore, they always would.

Now those two may have their problems, but one can never fault them for being lousy siblings. Though they are twins, there's nothing between them that might foster competition. No rivalry existed between Linus's math skills and Ophelia's literary interests. They both had a little trouble tripping over their own feet, but who wants to be better at that?

Do they ever annoy one another, you ask?

Of course not. They're flawless human beings. They love doing their chores too and getting out of bed at 5:00 a.m. to go running. The longer their school assignments are the better as far as Linus is concerned, and Ophelia loves nothing better than to get grades over 100 percent because of all the extra credit she completes! They're perfect teenagers, and you should pray your hardest that you behave just like them.

*That, my dears, is called sarcasm. In other words, you mean exactly the opposite of what is being said, which is usually revealed in one's tone of voice.*

While sarcasm is a form of irony, the best irony says exactly what it means, but the comparison and contrast is fully expressed. You would do well to know the difference between the two. So when an ambulance runs you over, or a digestive pill makes you regurgitate (throw up), you can say "How ironic!" And everyone will laugh at your misfortune. Get the picture?

In short, not only are the twins not remotely perfect,

there's nothing really special about the pair. Perhaps you wish Linus and Ophelia had magical powers at their disposal, could grow a hair suit when the moon is at the full, or actually were dead but walking around looking for live humans to consume, but they are, in and of themselves, as boring as you are, perhaps even more boring.

Ah, but where they live is far from the usual abode, and that is how they differ from the rest of society. It is not the fact that they live over a bookstore that sells only old books, a dark place that smells of old paper, mildewed leather, and the remnants of the flash flood that ripped through the town two months before. Or even that their aunt and uncle are, to put it kindly, eccentric oddballs. Their place on Rickshaw Street has a personality all its own, the brain of it housed all the way up under the eaves of the attic, which is exactly where the twins were lazing about on the tenth of August. Sweating profusely.

After a month of reading, they were ready for a change of scenery. They were ready for another adventure.

Linus decided sitting by the river would be cooler than spending the hottest part of the day up in the attic, as interesting as Cato Grubbs's lab equipment could be. The thought of firing up a Bunsen burner seemed as appealing as dipping one's feet in a slime-covered pond. *Not that I've ever done that, mind you. Heavens no!*

The twins slipped out of the bookshop, crossed Rickshaw Street, and walked between the stone pillars that flanked the entry to Paris Park, a beautiful place of lawns and trees that bordered the Bard River. They sat on a bench near the river, under the shade of a large Dutch Elm tree.

Kids from the Bard River Camp for Kids floated by them

on a canoe ride, all of them waving, including the counselors who invited the twins and Walter to the weekly bonfires.

Linus would refuse the invite tonight, he could tell you that! They waved back.

"I sure hope there's no bonfire," said Ophelia.

Walter bounded up in a pressed shirt and khaki shorts. He shamed Linus and Ophelia in appearance, but don't tell them I told you that. "Hi, guys."

He was getting the vernacular (local way of speaking) down. Walter wasn't one to stick out. He was naturally cool. Linus would never be cool, but he didn't mind.

Walter sat down next to them on the park bench. "Roasting, eh?"

"Tell me about it," said Ophelia.

"News?" asked Linus, lifting the hem of his T-shirt and wiping his face. His exposed ribs gleamed white in the shade of the elm tree that splayed its branches over the pathway.

"Definitely arson. Someone put lighter fluid in the dustbin and set it under the curtains in her loo."

They put the trashcan under the curtains in Madge's bathroom. So much for speaking American English. In his defense, he'd only been in Kingscross for two months.

"Who could have done it?" Ophelia tapped her chin. "Do you know of anybody that has anything against Madge?"

"I don't know of a single person that actually likes her," said Walter. "But not to that extreme."

"The damage?" asked Linus.

"The bathroom will have to be completely redone. At least that's what I overheard her saying to her brother on the phone this morning."

Ophelia sat up straight. "I didn't know she had a brother."

"His name is Johann. He said he would come home right away."

"Well, at least she's got family to help." Ophelia fanned herself with a flyer for Mr. Pine's Shoe Repair she'd found on the bench when she sat down.

"Or," said Walter, "maybe there's a reason her brother has stayed away for so long." He raised an eyebrow.

"Madrigal herself?" asked Linus.

"Would you blame him?" asked Walter. "Anyway, some people are coming to clean everything up today. Thankfully, it was rather contained." Walter stood up. "Let's go to the movies."

"Got a date." Linus stood too, jamming his hands in his shorts' pockets.

"I'm game," said Ophelia, wanting to tuck her hand in Walter's but knowing she would never dare do so.

Linus fetched Clarice from the parlor at the school and walked over to the ice cream shop where, true to form, Clarice—fair, slender Clarice—ate the eight-scoop sundae called The Trough all by herself.

You be the judge.

## three

# Good Psychology Makes
# for a Better Costume

*or* Let's Get This Party Started, Shall We?

The next day up in the attic, Ophelia cooled herself with an old Spanish fan she found in Uncle Augustus's costume collection, the breeze from the black and red half circle of fabric pushing her hair away from the sides of her face. Drops of perspiration slid down her temples and under her chin. "It's so hot up here."

Could anyone state the obvious any more obviously? No. And yet we all do this sort of thing all the time.

"Heat rises." Linus's straight blond hair hung in sweaty strands, some of it stuck to his forehead like cooked spaghetti. (*"Like cooked spaghetti" is a simile. A simile is when a writer compares one thing to something else using the words "like" or "as." If you want to get really highfalutin about it, a simile is a literary device that falls under the overall heading of "imagery." In other words, you make the reader conjure up an image in order to more precisely understand what you're actually talking about or to feel some kind of emotion. Whew! Somebody find me a handkerchief to wipe my brow—I'm as sweaty as the twins after all of that!*)

She rolled her eyes and fanned herself more forcefully. "Remind me why are we up here in the hottest part of the house?"

"He's downstairs."

Linus, a young man of few words, was in a constant state of figuring out how to pare down his speech even further. He'd tried doing ESP with everyone, but due to the fact that Ophelia was the only one that picked up his thoughts, he realized he wasn't really communicating to her purposefully so much as she could simply read his mind. Twins do that sort of thing, you know. A week before, he had decided to limit his responses to two words whenever possible. So far he was doing well, at least when their good friend Walter wasn't around.

Ophelia nodded from where she lay on a midnight blue velvet sofa with gold fringe most likely built a hundred years before. Everything inside the house on Rickshaw Street was originally bought by somebody else, and that somebody else was most likely no more. They were all what some people call antiques. Other people would call them moldy, disgusting dust traps. I'm not naming names. Tomorrow Uncle Augustus would throw his monthly party. He held one on the eleventh of every month, rain or shine, no matter the day of the week. The family all possessed a soft spot for the number eleven. It seemed to come up more than it should.

And it only took the twins over two months to realize it. *(I'm being sarcastic, remember?)*

Each party centered on a classic work of literature that went with their uncle's overall theme. Tomorrow was the "All for One and One for All Community Garden Party," in which they would don costumes from Uncle Augustus's collection and pretend they lived in the late sixteen-hundreds, in

France, during the exciting times of *The Three Musketeers*. Ophelia always read the books the parties revolved around. So far that summer she'd consumed *The Hunchback of Notre Dame* and *Moby Dick*. Ophelia is a reader, a good reader, which means she has a longer, more patient attention span than most young people today. She is not a dullard.

"He'll find us eventually, you know, Linus."

"Nope."

"I'd bet money he knows this attic is here. I'd bet money he knows we know about it too but is pretending he doesn't."

"How much?" Linus asked.

"Two bucks!"

"Nah."

Uncle Augustus kept them from being lazier than their natural predilection. (The way they tended to be when nobody cared one way or another.) In fact, they'd do no chores at all save for Augustus, who had them ripping up carpet and cleaning away sludge, as well as sweeping the front stoop and mowing the back garden.

"We'll wait," Linus said.

He turned on the swiveling library chair back to the experiment table before him. Linus decided he would uncover the secret to the enchanted circle, painted right there on the attic laboratory floor, if he did nothing else in life. He would be as great a scientist as his predecessor, the mysterious, some said mad, scientist, Cato Grubbs. He would find worlds nobody ever dreamed of. And the enchanted circle would lead the way.

*Oh dear. Now I suppose you will want to know all about this enchanted circle if you don't know about it already, in which case I have to ask you, "Why haven't you read the first two books in this series?" It would make this book somewhat easier for you to get a grip on. But you'll have to wait a bit. I could explain everything to you right now, or show you in real-time action when the circle comes to life at 11:11 p.m. the next day, as Uncle Augustus's party is still in full swing and the twins and Walter have been sent up to bed.*

*This writing tactic is known as "show, don't tell" and is one of the primary rules of good fiction. Far be it from me to break it like I did in chapter two, so you, dear ones, will have to wait. This adds an element of suspense as well, a veritable two-for-one special in literary methods. Writers love that sort of thing when it happens.*

Linus reached for what he called "the rainbow beaker." When held up to the light streaming in from the trefoil window (reminds one of a shamrock), the heavy liquid shone in a bright prism. He'd figured out a few weeks before that the rainbow beaker, or the formula therein, when combined with black powder number three, heated up to ninety-two degrees before noon, could bring inanimate objects from a book of one's choosing to the Real World of present day.

In the strange world of Linus and Ophelia, they'd come to know two worlds: Book World and Real World. You live in the Real World. As do I. *(Although sometimes I wonder about that.)* As do they. If you wake up and find yourself in the pages of a book, then do come see Linus. He has a lot of questions for you, and your knowledge would certainly speed up his experimentation. Or get to a good psychiatrist. Either one will do. *If you choose not to do anything, don't come crying to me. I warned you, didn't I?*

Of course, he'd told no one about his success in the laboratory of the building's former owner, Cato Grubbs, mad scientist, wearer of ruffles, and general troublemaker, with a personal goal of making himself rich making things difficult for everyone else. Some people are like that you know. I would call them busy bodies and instigators. You might call them drama queens. These types need no real reason to cause trouble other than the thrill of causing trouble. If you are a drama queen like Cato Grubbs, I suggest minding your own business and stop fiddling with the lives of those around you. Thank you.

As far as the rich part, Cato is greedy. Perhaps you know someone like that. Enough is never enough. Oh, they're insufferable!

Linus had been dodging Cato for the past four weeks. The scientist left threatening notes telling him to stop experimenting with his equipment and supplies. He looked at his sister, still sitting on the couch, and took a peek at the latest one.

*Ho, Boy!*

*You'll be sorry if you take 3 oz. of White powder no. 2 and combine it with a full bottle of milk of magnesia! I'd better never catch you doing that or revenge will be mine!*

Linus tried that very thing, naturally, and a little dancing flame resulted, lasting about three seconds before it waved a fiery little appendage, bowed, and disappeared. Linus then experienced a horrible case of indigestion and he'd used up all the milk of magnesia.

Cato always seems to add a dash more intrigue.

Ophelia wiped her forehead with her forearm just as their friend Walter entered the attic. "Hi, guys."

Walter's voice contained a strong London accent. His mother had enrolled him in The Pierce School for Young People, but had sent him off to the States early to keep him off the streets. He'd found the secret passageway one night that opened up in the Easterdays' bathroom, and soon the twins accepted him into their circle and they all became fast friends.

Sometimes people meet, and for no explicable reason, possess the feeling they've known one another for years. That's how the trio felt about each other.

Linus looked up from the experiment table. "Hi, Walt."

Walter walked over to Cato's desk and picked up a paperweight, a glass bubble of an object with a human molar inside, and threw it from hand to hand. "Has Uncle Auggie assigned costumes yet?"

"No," sighed Ophelia, setting aside her fan and sitting up. "We're just sitting here waiting for him to bellow."

Walter set down the paperweight and dropped to the floor for some push-ups. He was always doing that sort of thing and had the arms to show for it. Ophelia wouldn't admit it out loud to anyone, but she certainly admired those arms. After thirty or so, he stood up. "I've got a rather daft idea. Why don't we just go down, pick out our own costumes, and get it over with?"

Linus swiveled in his chair. "Good thinking."

Ophelia stood up. "Brilliant! Let's take matters into our own hands for once!"

## four

# Of Course a Man Can Wear Ruffles If He Wants To!

### *or* Never Get Caught Underdressed at an Adventure If You Know What's Good for You

𝓘t was good thinking. Usually Uncle Augustus picked out the worst costumes that made the boys feel especially silly. What red-blooded teenage male wants to wear tights on a summer evening? Or any day for that matter?

*People commonly think that because I work in the English department, I, Bartholomew Inkster, self-proclaimed Literary Fussbudget, would like to dress like people in Shakespearean times. Rubbish, I say!*

Walter was especially particular about his clothing. A reformed London street rat (never mention picking locks or pockets to him), he'd lately taken to having a well-groomed appearance. He showered at least once a day, even pressed his shorts. So old costumes? Poor Walter.

As for Linus, if it hasn't been washed a thousand times or is a white or blue T-shirt, you might just go ahead and put him in a suit of armor as far as he's concerned. Comfort at any cost. And the boy hates to do laundry. *I shudder to think of all that goes on in his laundry pile, I really do. Dust, grime, and moisture ganging up together to form ... well, ask your science teacher about spontaneous generation. It may not be as far-fetched a theory as one might think.*

"What era are we in this time?" Walter asked. He'd read *The Hunchback of Notre Dame* and *Moby Dick* after their first two adventures, but he had yet to read *The Three Musketeers*.

Thankfully, Uncle Augustus organized his costume collection by time period, and Ophelia started sliding hangers over one by one. "The late sixteen-hundreds," she told him. "It's a very fancy era too. Lots of lace and finery. I'm kind of excited!"

Linus shook his head. "Oh no."

Walter laughed. "Suddenly being a cabin boy in rags doesn't seem so bad."

"More comfortable," said Linus, remembering his last costume for the Whale of A Tale Seafood Party, the day the grouchy, speech-giving, "touched in the head" Captain Ahab made his appearance. *My heavens, that man could talk.* Not that Linus minded. Less pressure on him to utter a thing.

"That's for sure." Ophelia lifted off a suit of clothing and handed it to her brother.

He grimaced at the gold brocade vest, jacket, and knickers. A linen shirt with sleeves that could double as parachutes hung with it. "Oh man." In a bag hung black shoes with big buckles and some white stockings. The fabric was stiffer than a father's resolve when his teenage son asks for the car keys so he can go to a party.

She handed Walter his hanger.

"Brilliant!" he cried at the sight of an outfit any soldier of the time would have been proud to wear, black breeches and a blue velvet tabard (a smock-like over-garment) as well as a white shirt with a fancy collar. "I'll look like one of the musketeers."

"Thanks, Ophelia," Linus said with a tone. He shook his head and marveled at how inflection made all the difference, even to a mere thank-you. Why, you could say one thing and mean the exact opposite. Very economical word-wise. He liked it.

*Yes, my dears, Linus was employing sarcasm. Did you recognize it?*

Ophelia put a finger up to her lips as she picked through the gowns. "I am not going to be a servant this time. I'm going to be a lady."

She pulled out a full gown of silver blue, lace, bows, and pearls decorating it to such an extent it would render any pageant queen happier than a five-year-old with free rein in the candy aisle.

*The above description is a metaphor. Metaphor is like a simile only not using like or as. Brilliant, eh?*

Walter whistled. "You'll look beautiful in that, Ophelia."

She blushed. That's exactly what she wanted to hear.

The boys settled in Linus's cluttered blue room to sweat and play video games while Ophelia told Uncle Augustus they'd attended to matters themselves. She found him in the dining room making party favors.

"We picked out our costumes." Reaching for a satin ribbon to tie around a small bottle labeled "Much Needed Perfume," she sat down to help with the party favors.

*I certainly would not have wished to live in that time period when baths were a rare occurrence. Imagine the germs! The bugs! The grime! The germs! (Oh, I already said germs, didn't I?)*

He raised his eyebrows, his mouth turning down at the corners in appreciation. "Well good! I was hoping you'd take matters into your own hands eventually."

*Figures*, thought Ophelia, *we played right into his hands.*

She held up the bottle and chuckled. "I like this idea. I'm glad the costumes aren't from the time." She plugged her nose with finger and thumb. "P.U."

Uncle Augustus arched a brow. "How do you know they're not?" And he gave her a mysterious smile.

*Yes!* She thought. *I was right! He does know about the attic!*

*Oh no!* She frowned. One more adult in on the secret. This wasn't at all what they wanted.

"Where are the boys?" he asked.

"Upstairs in Linus's room."

"Be a dear and go get them, would you? I have a job for you to do."

The rest of the evening? Polishing the furniture, scrubbing the baseboards, polishing the silver, folding napkins, scrubbing toilets, anything Uncle Augustus could think of. By the time the trio fell in their beds, they felt as if they'd climbed a mountain.

## five

# It Takes a Fire to Create a Community

### or Sometimes You Have to Set a Tiger's Rooms on Fire in Order to Change Its Stripes

Ophelia powdered her face, applied some of Aunt Portia's bright red lipstick and pinned a fresh flower into the dark hair she'd curled in tight ringlets. Normally, she thought of herself as plain, but she found out what a lot of females do: a beautiful dress, well-coiffed hair, and a fresh flower bring out their God-given beauty.

When Ophelia appeared in the kitchen, ready to help serve the hors d'oeuvres (fancy little snack foods) created by Ronda, the caterer and hair dresser of the neighborhood, Walter sucked in his breath at the sight. He said nothing, however, just cleared his throat, grabbed a stack of napkins, and hurried into the dining room.

Ronda, wearing a slender black dress and a gold brocade apron, clapped her hands in delight. "You look gorgeous."

Speaking of gorgeous. Ronda, with her auburn hair and large eyes, provided a visual definition of that very word. (*Don't tell her I said so. I'll tell her you're being a drama queen.*)

Linus entered. "Silly clothing."

31

Ophelia laughed. "You look fancier than I do."

"All right, people." Ronda went over the roster of guests, the list of duties, and the time schedule. As they had at every other party, the trio went to work, carrying around trays of food and drink, providing general atmosphere to the party, and when they weren't serving, helping to slather spread on crackers, make up punch or lemonade, chop vegetables, or place food items onto toothpicks. Or being yelled at by Professor Birdwhistell from the philosophy department. *(None one in the English department can abide anybody in the philosophy department. Those philosophy people think they're the most insightful individuals on the planet. But we know better.)*

The professors of Kingscross University, the business people along Rickshaw Street, and neighbors and friends had all gone to great lengths to look like French nobility. Ringlets on the women, wigs on the men, sumptuous textiles and frills in a rainbow of color, even a crystal-topped cane or two appeared. Father Lou, invited for the first time, opted out on a full costume, instead sticking a large red, curling plume in his beret from his motorcycle club days. Ophelia thought he looked quite handsome in neat black slacks, a white shirt, and a leather vest.

But by nine o'clock, what with all that fabric on their bodies, all the guests had retreated to the back garden to escape the heat of the bookstore.

Everyone except Madrigal Pierce. She tapped Ophelia on the arm and ushered her to the living room where she sat her down and drilled her on her education in a manner of sorts. It was as if the fire hadn't happened at all.

"Well, now." She adjusted her skirts, skirts not in the

manner of the late sixteen-hundreds. Madrigal had also opted out of costuming, as she did not give one, two, or three hoots about such theatrics. In other words, Ms. Pierce is stuffy and haughty and will look down her nose at you even if you top her by a good eight inches. "By the looks of things around here, I suppose you're reading *The Three Musketeers*?"

"Yes, ma'am." Ophelia was learning how to handle Madrigal.

"And?"

"Well, I don't really know why Dumas (pronounced Doo-Mah) named it *The Three Musketeers*, as much of the story seems to be more about D'Artagnan, who wasn't even one of the musketeers for whom the novel was named."

D'Artagnan, the headstrong country boy who travels to Paris determined to be a musketeer, was good with his sword, and even better at romancing the ladies. A perfect literary hero.

A dreamy look settled into Madrigal's eyes. "Ah yes. D'Artagnan!" She made it sound more French.

*Well*, thought Ophelia. *The woman has a romantic bone in her body. I never would have guessed.*

"And your brother?" Madrigal asked. "What has he been reading?"

Of course, Ophelia knew. He'd been re-reading *It's All Reality: Traveling Through "Imaginary" Realms in Five Easy Steps*. But instead she said, "You'll have to ask him, Ms. Pierce." Linus would have to have a real conversation—just desserts for going into that fire!

Ms. Pierce stood up on her high-heeled shoes and gathered her fine shawl around her shoulders. "And so I shall!" she declared. When she got to the door, she turned. "Thank you for your help, Ophelia. I heard you called 9-1-1." And before Ophelia could say, "You're welcome," she'd clicked her way down the hall toward the stairs.

Professor Birdwistell's voice blustered in from the kitchen where he was telling Walter what a miserable waiter he made. The rotund little man, who was one of Uncle Augustus's best friends, should have been named Professor Sharpthistle or Toughgristle. Ophelia had never known someone so crabby. She was normally adept at finding at least something good in everyone, but for the past three months she'd only been able to come up with one thing. Professor Birdwistell did not smell.

The professor, who looked like a round little bird, puffed his chest out. "I keep wondering why Augustus allows you three to serve at his party. Children!" he spat out.

"We don't charge," said Walter. His neck began to turn red. "And furthermore—"

Ronda turned from the stove. "That's enough, Birdwistell. This is my kitchen and my crew, and if you don't like it, you know where the stairs are."

Ophelia wanted to cheer. Instead she hurried in. Birdwistell was one of Aunt Portia's best customers. "Hello, Professor! Lovely evening, isn't it? My you look handsome!"

On his way out of the room he awarded her compliment with a narrowing of his beady eyes. The man wasn't congenial, but that doesn't mean he's stupid. He knew a lie when he heard one.

"Way to go, Ronda," said Ophelia. "Really."

"Oh, I've been wanting to do that for a long time," she said.

Walter shook his head and swallowed his ire. "Thanks."

"Where's Linus?" asked Ophelia.

Nobody knew.

*Actually, Linus was somewhere. We always are, every single one of us, every single moment of every day. Although not always where we'd like to be, like when stuck at the top of a Ferris wheel. Oh my! I hate that, don't you? Even worse, going down basement steps in old houses. The dirt! The cobwebs!*

Linus had gone to the front steps of the bookshop to get away from the masses. Normally Linus didn't mind group settings. He spent so much time in his mind, spending time with others recharged his batteries. Whereas Ophelia, always the more outgoing of the two, needed to retreat to her bedroom with a good book to be able to face the writhing, germ-infested horde that is humanity.

Nevertheless, Linus's shoes bothered him. They were a bit too tight at the sides. When feet have to support that much height, they spread out a bit.

He removed his shoes, reaching down to squeeze his feet. *I do hope he thought to wash his hands when he went back inside. If he didn't, well, then I'm glad I was once again left off the guest list!*

He leaned against the stair railing and had just closed his eyes when the sound of a motor disturbed his peace.

*Figures.*

He looked up to see a green Westfalia van (VW camper van) pulling up to the curb in front of The Pierce School. A tall man, at least four inches taller than Linus and as thin as Ms. Pierce, climbed out of the driver's seat, walked around the vehicle, and opened the passenger door. He grabbed a messenger bag and a duffle bag.

*That's Madge's brother*, thought Linus. He carried himself just like her.

He strode through the school's garden gate.

*Ah-ha, dear reader! You're getting the picture, aren't you? No dullard, you! You know exactly who he is, don't you? The fire-setter! But the twins and Walter and Madrigal Pierce don't know, and you have no way to tell them, do you? Ha-hah!*

Ophelia slid her arm through Father Lou's and guided him into the kitchen. "Now I know you don't get haircuts very often, but you need to meet Ronda. She owns that little salon down the street. Hey, Ronda!"

Ronda turned around to face them from where she was sautéing something French at the stove, most likely something disgusting like snails. "Yes?"

"This is Father Lou, from across the street."

"Oh! At All Souls? Pleasure to make your acquaintance!"

A buzzer buzzed.

"So sorry! Time to get the lamb out of the oven."

"Nice to meet you too," said Father Lou.

His jaw could have been scraped off the floor.

*Well*, thought Ophelia, *this is interesting*.

Father Lou was so nice, such a good person, he deserved a good woman like Ronda. Ophelia didn't know why she hadn't thought of this before.

## six

# To Die Will Be an Awfully Big Adventure

### *or* We Don't Think About Death Like That Nowadays

Peter Pan quoted the above phrase, and to put it mildly, only someone who doesn't know better would mutter such utter nonsense.

*I don't know about you, my dears, but you can skip your awfully big adventures if it means never eating Thanksgiving dinner or feeling an autumn breeze glide across your face ever again. Do not sign me up for adventure dying. Please take note of that. If my cousin from Jersey City suggests going skydiving, please talk me out of it. Thank you.*

These days, most people think death is worth it if the sacrifice itself is worthy. For instance, one might consider someone pulling fifty people out of a plane only to sacrifice his own life to have died a worthy death. But if a person risks their life to get their fifteen minutes of fame on some reality television show, their death is not noble, it is stupid.

And one should not die a stupid death, even those reality television show dullards. *(I trust, because you are smart enough to be reading this book, that you will never be counted among them.)*

The reason death has become the topic of current

discussion is because blustery, passionate swordsmen from the sixteen-hundreds are a bit like Peter Pan. They get quite lackadaisical (not caring much one way or the other) about dying during their swordfights. And not just about their own deaths, oh no, but also about what constitutes a valuable human life.

Ophelia, Linus, and Walter were considering this very element as they waited for the enchanted circle to begin its display.

"I think d'Artagnan makes the most sense." Ophelia looked down at the two boys who were sitting on the floor by the couch.

"You would." Linus slid off his buckled shoes and yanked off his socks.

"Of course she would, mate." Walter took a look at the shiny, black leather boots he wore and decided to keep them on. "What lassie wouldn't pick the handsome hero to spring out of the pages? We may have come to love Captain Ahab and Quasimodo, but they weren't exactly charmers."

He winked at Ophelia, and Ophelia's heart sped up. She cleared her throat. "He just seems the most interesting. Let's face it, the other musketeers already know what they want out of life."

Linus leaned back. "Such as?"

Walter nodded. "Yeah. You might want to fill us in before the circle opens up."

"Aramis wants to be a priest. Porthos doesn't care much about anything as long as he has a lot of women to choose from and a great wardrobe. And Athos is perfectly content feeling haunted about love lost. D'Artagnan is young. He'll relate to us better. And besides, he is a hopeless romantic."

"So?" asked Linus. A one word response! He grinned.

Ophelia set her copy of *The Three Musketeers* beside her on the couch. "I was thinking that maybe we could use a little romantic interference."

Walter's mouth dropped open. "For who?"

Now it felt stupid. "Madrigal Pierce?"

Linus couldn't contain his laughter. *Madge? Loveable? Yeah, right.*

Walter rolled his eyes as if to say, *This is the weirdest idea you've ever had, Ophelia.*

"Okay, whatever." Ophelia looked at her watch. It was 11:10 p.m. "Ready?"

The guys nodded.

"Then let's see what the brash d'Artagnan will do with the world as it now is!"

She opened the book to the page she'd chosen that afternoon and set it in the middle of the circle. "Ready?"

The boys nodded.

Ophelia began the countdown. Starting with the number eleven, of course.

## seven

# Big Dresses Don't Always Cover a Multitude of Mistakes

### or Throwing a Twist into What Might Otherwise Be a Predictable Plot Is Never a Bad Thing

Oh dear, what happened next was unexpected, but even the most careful of people flub it up sometimes.

"... one ... go!"

Almost as if the circle was listening to Ophelia, it began to glow. A rainbow of colors pulsed on its curve, beginning with deep but vivid green into lapis blue, then indigo, violet. From crimson into a raging red, the circle pulsated an eye blistering orange, transitioned into a blinding yellow, then settled into the purest of white light.

After about three seconds, sparks rose quickly like fireworks, as if shooting from nozzles in the floor, hissing and popping and softly roaring in the small attic space. This was the fifth time the trio had seen the event.

"It never gets old," whispered Walter.

"Nope, never does," said Linus, forgetting his two-word minimum. Smoke, more like fog, settled in the circle's boundaries and a figure began to materialize in the middle, huddled in a heap of ... skirts?

Ophelia's mouth dropped open, her brows almost meeting together in the middle of her forehead in confusion. "Who ...?"

"That's not a bloke," said Walter as the sparks ceased and the smoke twisted like a tornado, then disappeared with an audible snap, leaving behind yet another figure!

Two?

The portal was closed and nobody in the room knew how to open it back up come what may.

Inside the circle sat the most beautiful woman anyone in the room had ever seen.

And that included Ronda, according to Linus. Now I didn't see this new woman for myself, but I rather have my doubts she could top Ronda. And next to her a dashing musketeer was passed out cold.

"Who is that?" asked Walter looking at the woman in horror.

"There are at least two beautiful women in the book. I don't know." Ophelia grabbed the book and ran her index finger down the page. "Oh no! I was so set on bringing d'Artagnan back during his journey to England—I wanted to warn him about Milady and Lord Buckingham's fate—I didn't notice she was on the page too." She hit her forehead with the heel of her hand. "Stupid! How could I not have noticed?"

"Who's Milady?" asked Linus, a sick feeling settling in his stomach.

"Pretty much the most evil person in the book. Well, next to the cardinal and the Count de Rochefort. But still."

"That's not good." Walter stood up and gazed at the pair.

"I can't even tell you how not good it is."

"And I assume that's d'Artagnan," he said, pointing to the male figure lying there as if he was taking the most delightful afternoon nap.

Ophelia nodded. "He's her enemy."

"Great," said Linus. "You've done it this time."

"Me?" Ophelia's face reddened. "You always leave the research up to me. Oh, Ophelia will read the book ... "

Milady, the Countess de Winter, opened her eyes, rubbed them a little, and smoothed the skirts of her yellow silk gown. Lace lined the low neckline and sleeves. Ribbons decorated the fancy dress, and embroidery so fine, only the best of dressmakers could be responsible for such mastery. She was the most beautiful woman any of them had ever seen, true, but it was more than physical appearance. The boys sucked in their breath. Ophelia blinked and blinked and blinked. Milady had the power to draw people in.

Ophelia knew, right there, she had made an enemy, a mortal one, if the Countess de Winter had anything to do with it.

D'Artagnan began to snore.

Milady's skin, the color of a pale pink rose, shone like a precious pearl in the candlelight. It was impossible to see the color of her eyes in the dim light of the flames, but Ophelia knew they were a clear blue. The pale yellow of her hair added to the fresh pallet of her appearance. The rosebud pink of her lips and the small feet in jeweled shoes peeking from beneath the folds of her skirt all attested to the fact that she was a wolf in sheep's clothing.

*A wolf in sheep's clothing is an oft-used expression for someone who is playing the part of a friend but who is, in fact, the enemy. Picture what happens when a wolf gets into the sheepfold. It isn't pretty, is it? Unless you're the wolf,*

*and then I suppose it's like dinner on the grounds. Much is a
matter of perspective, you see.*

Both Linus and Walter stepped forward and held out their
hand.

Milady took one in each of hers and rose easily to her
feet. "Why, thank you, my lord..." she nodded at Linus. "And
Captain," she said, nodding at Walter.

*So this is a captain's uniform*, he thought, hoping she
wouldn't realize he looked much too young for such a position.

"Welcome to Kingscross, Countess," said Ophelia. "You
are once again the prisoner of Great Britain."

Milady screwed up her face. "Great Britain? Wherever is
Great Britain?"

"England!" Walter practically shouted. "You are now a
prisoner of the crown."

Then he winked at Milady. Ophelia could hardly believe
her eyes. Linus said nothing.

"Who are you?" Milady asked Linus.

"Lord Easterday?" he said, turning his head frantically to
Ophelia who nodded.

"And I am his sister, Lady Ophelia Easterday. My brother
and I have been instructed to hold you here for the next three
days."

Without warning, the Countess de Winter lost all her
color and fainted into Walter's arms.

Now it was Ophelia's turn to roll her eyes. *Oh brother.*

## eight

# When It Rains It Pours

### *or* As If There Weren't Enough Strange People on Rickshaw Street

Walter picked up the noblewoman and laid her on the blue sofa. D'Artagnan still slept the all-encompassing slumber of youth.

"I couldn't believe she'd made the trip so easily!" Ophelia crossed her arms in front of her. "Both Quasimodo and Captain Ahab had a time of it."

"She must have a lot of fortitude," said Walter. "Unlike that guy." He pointed to d'Artagnan.

"You could call it that." Ophelia plopped down on the other end of the couch.

"That bad?" asked Linus.

"I mean, look at her." Walter touched a blond curl. "She looks like an angel."

"Madrigal Pierce is pretty too, Walt," said Ophelia. Good heavens, she was going to have a time convincing the boys of Milady's true nature.

"I know, but—"

"You should read the book. Believe me, she is not nice." Ophelia lowered her voice. "She may not even be asleep right now, guys. It would be just like her to pretend."

Linus sighed and sat down at the experiment table. This was going to take more than two words. "Do we need to bring anything from the book?"

"I don't know. This is going to be a mess. Trust me guys, containing the Countess de Winter is going to make keeping Captain Ahab under wraps seem like nothing. And then add d'Artagnan into the mix …"

Walter took another look at the perfect face asleep on the couch cushion and had to admit he thought Ophelia was wrong this time. Thankfully, he wasn't stupid enough to say so.

*Right now I'm setting up internal conflict within the group. Up until this point in our series the trio has always been united in their purpose, if not always their opinion, on how to accomplish it.*

*But introduce a beautiful woman, and a diabolical one at that, especially with teenage boys, and you can bet the story will get very, very interesting. Of course, Ophelia could simply be wrong about the countess.*

Linus and Walter left Milady in the care of Ophelia, who realized that yes, the French woman was actually asleep. She riffled through the pages of Dumas's novel, looking for a clue as to how she should proceed. Both Linus and Walter, completely ignorant of the story, promised to be no help at all in the grand plan of the next three days before the circle opened back up.

That's right. The trio had to keep this backstabbing, plotting, and scheming woman from making trouble of a monumental sort in the otherwise highly educated but highly boring town of Kingscross. (*If you want to see boring at its zenith, come to the English department where I work and talk with the professors. No better sleeping pill exists! And if you want to suck the heart and soul out of a good story, analyze it to death like they do.)*

A little less than sixty hours remained until 11:11 a.m., three days away, when the circle would open up again for the return trip. For the first time, Ophelia thought the acids between Book World and Real World which destroy characters who fail to pass back through may not be a bad proposition for someone like Milady. Ophelia could easily imagine this conniving, manipulating vixen melting away like the Wicked Witch of the West.

Ophelia looked over at d'Artagnan, his youthful face sweet in sleep. How in the world were they going to keep these two from getting into trouble and exposing the enchanted circle? She had no idea. Maybe they should forget about the circle come September.

So far, the outcomes of the traveling literary characters had been good for all involved, including what happened to Captain Ahab when he returned to the land of *Moby Dick*. Matters went as planned, according to Cato Grubbs, the mad scientist responsible for the circle to begin with, who accompanied the sea captain. Due to the trio's intervention, the crew of the *Pequod* made it back to Nantucket safely with a hold full of whale oil. Ahab decided to divorce himself from his greatest love, the sea, and move with his wife and son to the country, where he lived out his days in peace, eating no whale meat. In fact, he became quite the ardent vegetarian.

Ophelia fixed her gaze on the countess. But this traveler? Ophelia couldn't get one picture in her mind of how this would work out.

Inside the circle, d'Artagnan stirred. Ophelia hurried over just as he was opening his eyes.

"Why you are beautiful!" he said to her.

She blushed. *Maybe this wouldn't be so bad after all.* "I'm Ophelia Easterday. And you must be d'Artagnan."

He took her hand and kissed the back. "My reputation precedes me?"

"Yes," she said. *Oh my, but he was beautiful,* she thought. His hair caught the light of the candle with its silver blond strands. True, it could have stood a good washing, but there was time for that.

"How did I end up here? Where am I?" He looked around at the attic. "Can you tell me what is going on?"

His clear eyes were so earnest, something so trusting inside them, Ophelia realized she not only could, but should be straight with him about everything.

"How about getting out of this attic and going for a walk?" she asked.

"Lead the way, Miss Easterday." He noticed the Countess de Winter asleep on the couch. "How did she get here?" His eyes narrowed.

"I'll explain outside."

"Is it safe to leave her here alone?"

"She's passed out."

He set his jaw. "Good!"

*At this point, you might be wondering how someone from France and an American can be conversing together. Well, here's a fascinating little fact about the enchanted circle. Because Ophelia's translation was written in English, all the characters speak the same language. Brilliant, isn't it? And quite handy for all concerned.*

Linus decided he didn't want to go to bed just then. It was summer after all, and only midnight. So when Walter asked if he'd like to go back with him to the dorm, Linus said, "Sure thing."

They went back through the secret passage.

Once the Pierce family townhome, the building was quite ornate, and when the boys emerged from the closet, voices from down in the main hall wafted up the carved walnut steps and straight into their eardrums. They rushed to the top of the steps.

A man's voice spoke, but his back was to them. They only made out the words, "inheritance" and "about time."

"I wish I could hear what he's saying," said Walter.

Of course he did. Walter loved being in the know. Walter loved hearing the ins and outs of people's lives like we all do. The only difference is that Walter actually *admitted* he was nosy.

Madrigal spoke loudly and clearly. "Well, Johann, it's quite a surprise. After all this time you come back into the country and start demanding things, and from what you've said previously, I clearly thought you had no interest in this place."

" ... time ... finally ... mother and father always liked me—"

Madrigal cut him off. "I suggest a good night's sleep for all of us. You've had a long trip, and I'm tired too. I'll show you where you can sleep. Please forgive the mess the fire made."

Madrigal's high heels clicked on the marble floor of the entrance hall and her brother, most likely wearing comfortable shoes, followed almost without a sound.

"What do you think that was about?" Walter turned to Linus.

"Her brother?"

They set off down the hall to Walter's room.

"Sounds like it could be. He sure stands like she does." Walter swung open the door to a small chamber with two single beds, one empty. Two dressers, one empty. Two closets, one empty. One bookshelf, completely filled.

"Hey!" a voice whispered down the hallway just as the boys stepped into Walter's room.

Linus backed out and peered down the hall, his face deepening to a shade of red. "Hi, Clarice."

Clarice stayed at the school for the summer because her parents had better things to do with their time than spend it with their daughter, who would have just as soon been away from them. In this, she and Linus had much in common. She pulled her long blond hair back into a ponytail. "I was just going for a run."

*She was the athletic type. Don't try to understand it, just know it takes all kinds to make a world.*

"Want to come?" she asked Linus.

"Sure." He turned to Walter. "Okay?"

"Oh, don't mind me. I've got a book to read." He waved them off.

Ophelia took d'Artagnan straight to the manse. Father Lou remained true to his usual, unflappable nature. It was almost as if he saw people like d'Artagnan traipse through his kitchen at midnight three days a week. "Tell me everything," he said, pulling out a chair for the new guest.

Ophelia introduced the men to one another.

"Are you hungry?" Father Lou asked the latest traveler through the portal.

"Famished."

"Go ahead and put your sword by the door. Feel free to take off your boots." He turned to the refrigerator and pulled out the makings for a turkey sandwich.

"What is that lighted box? Is it witchcraft?" d'Artagnan said, pointing to the refrigerator.

"Not hardly. We'll explain in a minute," said Father Lou. "Go ahead, Ophelia."

"Before I begin," Ophelia said, "I need to ask, have you ever read *The Three Musketeers*?"

"Yes." Father Lou took two slices of bread from out of the bag.

"Oh, thank goodness!"

"You know of the musketeers?" asked d'Artagnan. "Magnificent!"

Ophelia sat. "Yes, they are. But you are destined to be even greater."

"Surely not!"

"Just wait and see," said Father Lou.

"How is it you know so much about me?" asked the musketeer.

"Let me explain," Ophelia said.

"And while you are explaining, miss, can you tell me what those moving contraptions are called? No horses? The streets are clean. And those lights, high up on the tree trunks. What are they?"

*It's going to be a long night*, thought Ophelia. "I'll be happy to get to that, but first let me tell you how you got to be here." She looked at Father Lou. "All right. Let me just say we made a mistake and the Countess de Winter came through as well."

"Oh dear." The priest shook his head.

"Pah!" said d'Artagnan. "That woman!"

"Don't worry, son," he said, moving over to lay a hand on the younger man's shoulder. "It gets worse."

Ophelia suppressed a smile. "All right. Here goes." She promised herself that in the next month she would write down this speech instead of stumbling over it time after time.

In the middle of her explanation, Father Lou set the sandwich in front of his guest. Turkey on whole wheat with Provolone cheese, mayonnaise, Dijon mustard, and crisp lettuce. D'Artagnan took one bite and proclaimed it, "Magnificent!"

Amazing what a great sandwich will do, isn't it? If Father Lou had made liverwurst on pumpernickle with thinly sliced onion and a little butter, d'Artagnan might just have fainted from the delights contained therein!

She finished the story after another five minutes. He shook his head. "How do I know you're telling me the truth?"

Both Ophelia and Father Lou then told him more about his life than he would have told anybody himself.

"All right! All right! Enough!" he cried. "When the tale is told to my ears, I can barely listen to my own foolishness." He wiped his mouth. "Am I really that rash?"

Ophelia and Father Lou nodded.

"Sorry about that, son," Father Lou said. "You're young. Chalk it up to too much passion and too little experience."

"And then you throw a sword into that mix," said Ophelia.

Father Lou stood up. "How about we all settle in for the night? Care to stay over here? It's much cooler."

"Anywhere would be better than that attic." D'Artagnan nodded to Father Lou with appreciation. "Have a bit of time to answer some questions, Father? I saw some strange things along the side of the streets, huge lumpish carriages and not a horse in sight."

"Of course."

Ophelia sighed with relief. God bless people like Father Lou. Feeling satisfied d'Artagnan wasn't going anywhere, she ran back across the street, relieved to have one character settled in for the night. And now, back to Milady. Hopefully she was still passed out.

Oh, such wishful thinking, Ophelia!

Clarice grabbed Linus's hand and led him down the hall toward the back stairs of the building knowing Ms. Pierce would be none the wiser that she was leaving well after curfew.

They walked across Rickshaw Street and between the stone gateposts of Paris Park, the large city park that ran alongside the Bard River. Clarice escorted Linus over to a spot on the riverbank where a large flat rock sat half in the water, half out.

She sat. Linus sat.

"I didn't really want to run. I just wanted to see you."

"Okay." Linus grimaced. He wouldn't have minded his answers being more than two words with Clarice, but unfortunately, the ways of love stole from his vocabulary and usually subtracted one word from his answers.

*I must seem like a caveman.*

"So, I was walking by your house a little while ago and I saw the weirdest lights coming out of the attic window, the one that has the three circles?"

"Trefoil."

"Trefoil?"

"Window."

"Trefoil window?"

"Yup."

*Can I seem more stupid?*

"So anyway, what was that all about?" She reached into the pocket of her gym shorts and pulled out a pack of gum. Holding it out to him—he took a stick—she raised her eyebrows. "Well?"

He sighed. "Ophelia."

"Did she do something?"

He shook his head.

"Oh, I should ask her?"

"Uh-huh."

"Okay. Say no more."

The old Clarice was back, the Clarice that had sat with him for the past month under shade trees in this park, reading while he tried to teach himself Calculus II (I don't recommend that); the Clarice who ordered three hotdogs at the stand on the corner and ate them with Linus, saying nothing; the Clarice who slaughtered him in tennis every time and never rubbed it in.

He'd become used to her quiet presence the past few weeks.

So they simply sat by the river, hand in hand now, breathing in the heated air of August, listening to the sound of crickets and the blurp of frogs, and the sound of a muffled scream borne on the hot wind.

"What was that?" asked Clarice.

"Probably nothing," said Linus.

She shrugged. "Okay."

Oh dear. Poor Ophelia.

## nine

# Even Crabby People Don't Deserve to Lose Everything They Love

### *or* The Problem Firmly Established, Nobody Yet Has an Idea What to Do

*That device I just employed, ending the chapter with such a dramatic, mysterious piece of news, is called a hook. It's called a hook because it's designed to hook you, like a fish on a line, so you'll have no choice but to turn the page and start the next chapter.*

*Now you know why you didn't put this book down and pick up the video game controller. Ingenious, isn't it? Of course a parent might have been reading this with you and bedtime is bedtime and all that. Spoil-sport. But we won't hold it against them. This time.*

Poor Ophelia, having fallen asleep at the worktable, was jerked to consciousness with a knife, a stiletto (a smaller

knife with a long, slender blade honed to a needle-sharp point) to be precise, pressed to her throat. And do you know who held the knife?

Of course you do.

"Now, be silent and tell me why I'm here," hissed Milady, who clearly had the knife hidden somewhere on her person, most likely strapped to her leg.

Ophelia's eyes darted around the room. Why did she take d'Artagnan over to Father Lou? He would have come in handy just then. "Get that knife away from my throat and you've got yourself a deal."

It took every bit of courage her fourteen years of experience had ever deposited into her psyche for Ophelia to remain calm. But this wasn't her first adventure with a literary character, and she was determined to make sure it wasn't going to be her last.

"You can keep hold of it, just not against my throat," Ophelia said calmly, while inside she was screaming, *I've got a knife ... at my throat!*

"All right." Milady backed away. "But if you try anything ... I'll attack."

*Whew!* "Oh, I know you will, Countess."

A gleam of curiosity shone from her eyes. "And how so?"

"Believe me. I know more about you than you do about me."

Here we go again!

"Would you care to illuminate me?" She crossed her arms over her chest, her movement fluid and graceful.

Ophelia did the same, her movement anything but. "I'll just say this so you know who you're dealing with. I know your left shoulder bears a branding in the shape of a fleur de lis."

The blue eyes widened. "No! You could not possibly!"

Ophelia stood to her feet. "No secret can be kept forever, Countess."

"How much?"

"I'm a lady, madam. I cannot be bribed." Ophelia, in truth, was having the time of her life now that the knife wasn't positioned against her jugular vein. No one could accuse her of being a drama queen normally, but perhaps she was just saving it all up for such a time as this.

"Why am I being held captive?"

"You have conspired to kill Lord Buckingham, the prime minister of England."

That wasn't actually accurate. At this point in the novel, the Countess de Winter was trying to implicate the queen of France who was madly in love with Lord Buckingham.

"That isn't true!" The woman didn't blink, flinch, or pale.

"If we find nothing against you in three days' time, you'll be free to go about your business."

The countess cocked an eyebrow. "You say I'm in England? You don't sound like any Englishwoman I've ever heard."

"Have you been to Kingscross in"—Ophelia flipped through her geographical brain file in the section labeled 'Great Britain'—"Cornwall?"

"No." Milady lifted her chin.

"Well, good. That's where we are now. And this is how we speak."

"But how did I get here? Last I knew I was—"

"You were given a heavy sleeping tonic and brought here. You live quite the adventurous life, Countess. Must be exciting being an operative of Cardinal Richelieu."

"Ha!" the countess laughed. "You know that?"

And Ophelia knew her plan right then. The old adage came to mind. Keep your friends close and your enemies closer.

She leaned forward, her lips close to Milady's ear. "Le Comte de Rochefort ... is ... my mother's cousin. As long as you stay with me, Lady, you are safe."

"What about the others?"

"The young men? My brother is trustworthy. The other? He will act like he is your friend only to draw you in. Do not let your vanity believe him for one second." Ophelia hadn't liked the way Walter seemed so taken by Milady. This ought to thwart his chances. *Wait! Was Ophelia acting like Milady?*

Now that made the countess lose her color. Men not really trying to win her favor? Oh, horror of horrors!

"Now how about a little food?" Ophelia asked. "I'm sure you must be hungry after the journey."

"Indeed I am." Milady's face cleared. Obviously now was not the time for her to do anything other than get a clearer picture of what was truly going on. The woman was patient in her dark machinations (evil plans), if nothing else.

"I'll be right back with some food."

Ophelia exited the room, shutting the door and jiggling the handle as though locking it, and hoping the Countess de Winter wouldn't try to leave.

In *The Three Musketeers*, the Comte (the French word for Count) de Rochefort plays henchman to Cardinal Richelieu, the most powerful man in France at the time. In other words, he took care of the cardinal's dirty work. (*A cardinal is a person with a lot of power in the church. Thankfully, cardinals* tend to shy away from using heads of state such as kings, queens, and presidents as puppets these days.) The cardinal had it in for the queen and used the comte and Milady, the Countess de Winter, to try to discredit the queen in the eyes of the king. Cardinal Richelieu feared the queen might have too much sway with her husband, who, quite frankly, wasn't a very good ruler in his own right (one might wonder if he was one of the dullards), and the cardinal wanted all the influence for himself.

In other words, Cardinal Richelieu was power hungry, so power hungry he didn't mind using anyone to accomplish his means, including beautiful countesses.

Ophelia's mind was spinning like a top as she prepared a plate of leftovers from the party, including the little cream puffs (some extra for herself). She knew she had to have a serious discussion with Walter. It was obvious her friend was bowled over by the countess's beauty. Who wouldn't be?

As she was laying down the final hors d'oeuvre, a puff pastry filled with patè, Linus and Clarice entered the kitchen.

Ophelia started. What was her brother thinking? And tonight of all nights! "Well, hello, Clarice."

"Hi, Ophelia. So, you'll want to know why I'm here." Direct as ever, she continued. "It's because I have a question, and your brother might explode if he has to answer it."

Her tone hardly sounded critical. Obviously, she thought Linus's inability to communicate was the sweetest, cutest thing ever.

Clarice backed up to the counter, pressed the palms of her hands behind her and sprung up to sit with her legs dangling. "Oh, wow! Can I have some of those leftovers?"

"Let me," said Linus, springing to action. Boy would Aunt Portia and Uncle Auggie wonder where all the food went, because once Clarice got going, it was a feeding frenzy. Linus liked that about her.

*A word to you young ladies, the males of the species like females who eat. It lets us know you're healthy. So go ahead and fill your plate with good things. We'd hate for you to starve yourself on our accounts. But do make sure you don't leave your dishes hanging about for days. Some of us can't abide the thought of that much bacteria building up. Not many of us, but some. Thank you very much for your cooperation.*

"What were all those lights about earlier? I saw them from the attic window."

Ophelia shot her brother a glare.

He shrugged, a helpless expression plastered on his face.

"Hold on, Clarice." She grabbed her brother by the crook of his arm and dragged him to the dining room. "What should we do? Do you think she's safe enough to let in on the secret?"

"I don't know."

"Then she's not."

Ophelia entered the kitchen. "Okay, here's the deal. Linus here has been doing experiments with the lab equipment that was left up there by the former resident."

"Why didn't you tell me that?"

"Because he used to be made fun of for being so ..."

"Scientific?" Clarice supplied.

"Exactly!"

"But I love that you're scientific, Linus!"

Reddening, Linus handed her the plate of food, a heaping plate of food.

Clarice picked up a tiny tart filled with caramelized onions and asparagus. She bit down. "Mmm! Okay, so I know you heard the last part of the conversation between Madrigal and her brother." So Clarice was spying too.

"Yeah."

"What conversation?" asked Ophelia. She knew she had to get the food up to Milady, but she couldn't just leave. There was news. And Clarice knew her well enough to know that Ophelia was as curious—nosy—as Walter. It would raise a question or two in Clarice's mind if she bolted just then.

Clarice continued. "Apparently, Madrigal's estranged brother returned from overseas where he's been living for the past twenty years."

"How come?" asked Ophelia.

"She hasn't heard from him for ten years, and here he shows up so soon after the fire." She popped another tart into her mouth, chewing it completely—making Ophelia want to scream in impatience—before swallowing and continuing on with the story.

"Anyway, from what I could hear from the drawing room, he wants his share of the family home. Apparently, he met someone where he lives in Japan, and he wants to have the money for their marriage."

Ophelia said, "But then Ms. Pierce will be forced to sell the school. She loves that place."

"Yep. It's her whole life." Clarice hopped down. "So as I see it, we have to think of a way to scare Johann straight back to Japan."

"We?" asked Ophelia.

Clarice tucked her arm into Linus's. "We?" she asked him.

"We," agreed Ophelia. "We'll set up a plan tomorrow."

When Ophelia entered the attic, Milady had fallen asleep, a copy of *The Three Musketeers* in her hand.

## ten

# The Best Laid Plans of Mice and Men Are Most Likely Infinitely Better than the Best Laid Plans of Ophelia Julia Easterday

The next morning, Walter and Ophelia, Linus keeping guard on Milady, headed across the street to All Souls Episcopal Church to have a conference with Father Lou and to check on d'Artagnan. The ponytailed, motorcycle-riding priest had been in on the enchanted circle since Quasimodo, the hunchback of Notre Dame, their first transport arrived.

They filed into the rectory (the house provided by the church for its clergy) and sat down at the small kitchen table covered with a white cloth. Father Lou knows how to bleach a tablecloth, a quality much to be admired. The morning sun illuminated the linen like a spotlight, and already the room was warming up well above comfort level. Due to the heat, his usual pot of tea was lemonade.

"Sorry about the heat this morning," Father Lou said. "I'm trying to save the church money by keeping the AC off as much as possible."

The trio had been going to All Souls since June, and to put it nicely, they were by far the youngest people in the congregation. However, the elderly members doted on them, a nice thing to happen to anyone. They never sat through a service without candy being passed to them from all directions. It was like Valentine's Day every Sunday.

"Where's d'Artagnan?" Ophelia added extra sugar to the sour lemonade.

"He's still asleep," Father Lou said. "Probably for the best."

"No kidding," said Walter.

"How's the other traveler?" Father Lou set a plate of chocolate chip cookies on the table and sat down.

Ophelia spooned even more sugar into her lemonade, explaining all the while about Madrigal's dilemma.

"Oh, wow," said Father Lou, lifting his glass and taking a sip. "I can't imagine the neighborhood without the school around."

"Me either," said Ophelia.

"And if it closes, I'll be sent back home." Walter picked up his glass and traced rings with his forefinger in the condensation.

Ophelia looked at Walter in horror. "I didn't think about that! Oh, Walter!"

Walter took a sip and sighed. "No use worrying about it—yet."

"So," said Ophelia, "I'm wondering if we could use Lady de Winter and d'Artagnan in some way."

Father Lou scratched his tattooed arm. (He'd come to the ministry later in life.) "Let me think about it, Ophelia. I'm sure we can come up with something to scare Johann away."

"All right," Ophelia said.

Deciding that Linus shouldn't be responsible for the countess much longer, they all left, and as they walked, Ophelia whispered to the priest, "She has that way about her."

"I realize how dangerous she is." He patted her shoulder. Father Lou knew all about people who liked doing the wrong thing, being a former bounty hunter (That is, someone who goes after people who are wanted by the law and brings them in to the authorities. For a price, or, as the title says, a bounty.).

"Because I don't think the boys realize."

He laughed. "That stands to reason. It will be all right."

Ophelia nodded. But somehow, she doubted Father Lou's optimism. It was never that easy when the enchanted circle was involved.

"By the way, Father. How long has it been since you've had a date?"

"You don't even want to know."

She stepped out the door, shutting it just as Father Lou asked, "Why?"


Ophelia heard Milady's giggles as she trod up the staircase to the attic. *Already busy charming the boys*, she thought.

On her way home from the rectory, she stopped at Ronda's and borrowed some adult women's clothing. She also talked about her visit to Father Lou. How kind Father Lou was. How good with children. And "He's kinda cute," she said. "For an old guy." Best to start laying the groundwork. Truth was, Ronda and Father Lou would make a good couple, Ophelia figured. *I suppose people who work in the English department at Kingscross University aren't good enough for beautiful cosmetologists, eh, Miss Easterday?*

"Hello, everybody!" Ophelia said as cheerfully as she could.

Milady, seated on the sofa, knit her brows. "What is this

change of garb, Lady Ophelia?" She pointed to Ophelia's skirt, her favorite, a flowing longer skirt of pink cotton. "Each of you seemed so familiar yesterday, and now look at you all! Peasants!" She glanced at the boys. "But delightful peasants I must add."

They laughed. Ha, ha, haaaah! Ophelia wanted to knock their heads together, but instead just muttered "Oh, brother," underneath her breath, and who can blame her, really?

"I have something to tell you. Something you may not believe," Ophelia said.

Walter's gaze snapped to Ophelia. "Now? Really?"

Ophelia knew they couldn't keep Milady hostage forever. A woman like Milady was always in control. She hoped to flummox (confuse) her, to put her at odds with her surroundings, and so gain the ability to manipulate her more effectively.

*Yes, my dears, Ophelia can be that calculating. She is not a dullard. Never has been, and never will be. You know how I know this? Because she's not in front of a glowing screen for numerous hours each day. I'm sure you're not either.*

She sat down on the attic floor and reached for *The Three Musketeers* from where it sat on the experiment table. Both Walter and Linus looked worried.

A strange scent, not unpleasant, hit her nose. "What's that smell?"

Walter dropped to the floor and did push-ups immediately.

"Oh." Ophelia laughed. He was wearing cologne. This could get drastic.

*This seems to be going well.* Ophelia came toward the end of the story. "And so, you see, we realized we can bring characters from books to life. The mad scientist, Cato Grubbs, whose lab this used to be, left detailed notes behind, thank goodness."

"Well, I suppose I should be honored you chose me," said Milady.

"Oh, we didn't! We thought we were just bringing d'Artagnan over!"

"You chose d'Artagnan? That brash young man? Ha!"

"Why do you say that?"

"The musketeer has no idea what he wants, which makes him all the easier to use. Be wary. He will fall in love with you, and then when you aren't as exciting, he will move onto someone else." If she could have spat, she most likely would have.

Suddenly, Ophelia saw a real woman behind the scheming eyes of the Countess de Winter. "So, you figured you might as well use him right back?"

"A woman does what she has to do to survive, Lady Ophelia."

"Just call me Ophelia, and they're just Walter and Linus." She thumbed in the boys' direction.

Well, if she wanted to disconcert (freak out) Lady de Winter, she wasn't doing such a hot job, was she?

"So when do I go back, Ophelia, or do I? And you said I'm over three hundred years into the future. And am I actually real?"

"Do you feel real?" asked Walter.

She rubbed her right arm with her left hand. "Of course."

Ophelia breathed in through her nose. "Yes. You're real. Well, here's the way it works."

"I'm hungry," said Linus.

"Why don't you get us all some lunch?" asked Ophelia. "Hot dogs?"

Milady didn't even blink. "I suppose I should not even ask what those are."

"Sausages," said Walter.

"Well, why don't you simply call them sausages?"

"Why do you call a cookie a Madeleine?" asked Ophelia.

"What's a cookie?"

"Never mind. Listen, there's more. If you don't get back in the circle at 11:11 the morning after next, you'll die."

Milady laughed.

*Well, that's a new reaction*, thought Ophelia. The woman was unflappable.

"She's serious, Milady," said Walter. "It's true."

She turned to Walter and batted her eyelashes. "Are you sure?"

*Ugh!* Ophelia wanted to scream. The countess was clearly one of those women who only listened to men. Then again, from where she came, men were the only ones whose opinions counted.

Maybe it was his accent.

"Yes, ma'am. And according to the notes, it's much like being thrown into a vat of hydrochloric acid. Very, very painful to melt away like that."

Milady didn't ask what hydrochloric acid was. She got Walter's drift and that was most likely enough.

"So far we've been able to send everyone back on time." Walter sat next to her on the sofa. "Let me give you a piece of advice. You'd be wise to listen to Ophelia. She's the smart one among us and honestly, we can make the next few days a lot of fun for you, show you around Kingscross, or you can try to go it on your own and make life a lot more difficult and risk not getting back into the circle on time."

Ophelia pulled Ronda's clothes out of her knapsack. "I've got some clothing in our style. We have a lot to show you. Your mind will be blown!"

"Pardon?"

"You won't believe what it's like now," said Walter.

Several minutes later, Linus entered, his hands full of hot dogs. "Let's eat."

Now you might be thinking the Countess de Winter accepted the bizarre with an unrealistic ease. But if you've read *The Three Musketeers*, you might also be thinking she didn't believe a word they were saying. And who, really, could blame her?

## eleven

# If a Villain Can't Be Well-Developed, She Might As Well Be Well-Dressed

Milady had to admit that a hot dog wasn't a bad thing despite its name. But it took some real persuasion on Ophelia's part to get her to put on Ronda's clothing.

"I'll tell you one thing"—she held up a pink T-shirt—"you'll be a lot cooler in this."

"It's no better than a chemise!" Apparently, even a woman as dubious as Milady could be shocked.

Basically, a chemise is a woman's undershirt from olden times.

"It's perfectly proper these days, I assure you, Milady."

Milady sat on Ophelia's bed. Walter and Linus had gone to meet Clarice over at The Pierce School to see what was happening with Madrigal and Johann. Ophelia wasn't sure if she should let the countess in on what was happening, or just let her do what came naturally—allure men into thinking she was the most beautiful thing this planet had ever produced, and that included roses, snow-capped mountains majesty, and the perfect slice of New York pizza.

She decided to let events play out naturally at first and step in later if necessary. Good advice to all of us. Most of the time, if we wait, the situation clears itself up and we did not make fools of ourselves.

"This is indecent!" the countess cried when Ophelia held up a gypsy skirt covered with a light rainbow of paisley print. "Perhaps I should just stay where I am."

Never before had Ophelia had to convince a character like this to get out of the attic. Maybe she *should* just let her stay here. "You know, Milady, if you don't put these clothes on, you'll have to stay up here in the heat. There's a lovely park across the street, with a river, and benches. It's called Paris Park."

The blue eyes lit up. "Yes? Paris is wonderful."

"Yes. Now let me help you into these things and we'll go over and sit in the breeze. If you can't stand it, we'll come right back. I promise."

The countess looked doubtful.

For some reason, Ophelia felt sorry for her suddenly. "It will be all right. You'll see."

"Will the young men be coming?"

*Ugh! Not again!* "They'll be joining us later."

She nodded once. "Well, then. Help me into this garb." She lifted the pink shirt. "What do you call this again?"

"A T-shirt."

"Oh! So we're having tea at the park?"

"No."

"Then why—"

"I don't know."

It appeared there was much Ophelia didn't know about her own world. She hadn't realized it until now. She supposed she should be grateful to the wicked Milady for bringing questions to the surface.

No. Let's not get silly, Ophelia.

"Would you like a bath first?" Ophelia asked. She remembered the time period from which Milady came, a time when people took baths once a year and used a lot of perfume in the between time.

*I shudder to think of it. Imagine the sweat collecting and drying, collecting and drying. And the clothing must have become stiff with—moving right along!*

"I might as well. These clothes leave everything out in the open. I should probably smell nice."

"Right."

It appeared one *could* teach an old dog new tricks. Either that or Milady was extremely adaptable.

*When reading novels, particularly those written long ago, we normally see only part of the character. After all, what novelist has time to really and truly think up an entire life, much less write it all down! All those days, all those months, all those years! Walking to the store. Going to movie after movie. And school—endless days of school. Doing the dishes. Tying shoes. Brushing teeth. Answering cell phones. Mopping. Sweeping. Scrubbing. My goodness.*

*Nowadays, villains are portrayed with more nuances (angles or sides) so that at the very least, the reader can somewhat understand how they got to be so evil, the reader can somehow remember that the antagonist was once born a sweet little baby, as sweet as you once were to your own mother and father.*

*However, on each page that Milady appears in* The Three Musketeers, *she is, simply put, a bad person. Never once does Dumas give us a glimpse of what series of events brought her to the point where she didn't care who lived, who died, as long as she survived and did so with all she desired intact.*

The brand on her arm was for stealing the Communion chalice and patens from the local parish. Who steals from a church? But more importantly, why? Dumas never says. One must take it that he was trying to establish she was "born bad." But Ophelia realized that even Milady was once a toddler with innocent blue eyes, running around the yard and trying to ride the dog or flushing the toilet over and over again, which is what Milady did when Ophelia showed her how the toilet worked. Oh, the luxuries we all take for granted!

Ophelia had run the bath *(Milady was delighted by the easy availability of hot water, just like Captain Ahab and Quasimodo)* and was now sitting outside the bathroom door, wondering, as we would with real people, how the Countess de Winter ended up so cruel. Surely it wasn't all her fault, was it?

Oh no! Ophelia gasped. She was being drawn into Milady's spell! How could she have been so stupid?

Or was she?

Suddenly Ophelia understood how d'Artagnan was utterly fooled (later on in the book, of course), turning his back on the sweet, beautiful maid to the queen of France to be with the countess. *And certainly, it's nothing new for someone to confuse outward beauty with goodness. We're always so surprised when a beauty is terrible, and worse yet, when a beautiful person dies, we are all the more sad for it, as if us plain folks' lives are less worthy to be lived. Don't do that. It's terrible to judge a life on that basis. If you don't like that, take it up with the administration and your local minister. Thank you.*

"I'm finished!" Milady cried. "You may come dry and dress me now!"

Ophelia jumped to her feet and called through the door. "I'm not your servant, Milady. We don't do that sort of thing anymore around here. The towel is hanging on the hook at the back of the door and your clothes are right there on the counter by the sink. I will do your hair for you, however. You absolutely cannot go out looking like that!"

"You say that as if my hair is a bad thing," she retorted.

"It is, Milady."

"Oooh!" Milady shot out.

Ophelia smiled. And she was right. The countess had removed her wig—which I would have burned right away—and her hair underneath was matted and greasy. "I'll help you wash it here at the sink."

Thankfully it was still the same golden color once it had been washed. *And I'll just say this once, I'm glad it was Ophelia's job and not mine. I don't know how hairdressers do it, day after day, sticking their fingers against people's scalps. They're saints, I tell you. Saints!*

Blond hair in a simple ponytail, Ronda's free-spirited garb hiding her slender body, Milady could hold her own in the present day as well. She looked at herself in the mirror and frowned. "Disgusting!"

"No, no!" cried Walter a bit too enthusiastically. "Hardly. For our time period, you're perfect."

She beamed and caressed his cheek with her hand. "What a lovely lad you are."

He blushed.

Ophelia felt a little nauseous.

They hurried Milady down the steps, hoping to make it through the kitchen and out the back door with Aunt Portia and Uncle Augustus none the wiser.

No such luck.

At the top of the steps leading down to the bookshop, Aunt Portia stood.

*Oh, you'd love Portia Easterday, and I can say that without a modicum—little bit—of doubt. She looks on the world in her own way, at her own pace, and for her own peace of mind.* Portia and her brother Augustus's parents were as eccentric as Linus and Ophelia's parents, but much more attentive. They owned a small theater and showed plays always starring, you guessed it, themselves and their pair of twins. That's what the family lore says anyway. It isn't any wonder their children have a flair for the dramatic and have a bit of a hard time with what is real and what isn't. Then again, who doesn't?

Delightfully, however, Portia didn't quite learn the rules of the world, but wasn't harmed one whit (little bit) because of it. She thought everyone was a friend until they proved otherwise, and there wasn't a color combination that failed to be an option. She wore rhinestones no matter the time of day and ate handfuls of gummie bears when she thought no one was looking.

Her bright pink lips broadened with a smile, and her apricot-colored frizz of a hairdo vibrated when she said, "Well, well! Who have we here? I had no idea we had a visitor!" She clapped her hands, all eight rings she wore—she decided to wear all her good rings so nobody would steal them—clinking together.

Linus said, "The Countess de Winter."

If Portia was surprised, she didn't show it. "Come all the way from Paris! Well, my stars! Welcome to Kingscross!"

Milady's glance burgeoned with mistrust. "Yes ..."

"Wonderful!" She turned to Ophelia. "Surely you're bringing our guest to dinner, and by all means, use the guest room this time!"

"What's for dinner?" asked Walter.

"We're going green today! Broccoli, peas, salad, and fried green tomatoes. You'll love it."

Walter had heard what they were serving at the school, some fried meat cutlet (referred to as mystery meat at college cafeterias everywhere) and canned green beans, and this was a far sight better.

Be glad you don't have to eat the food at The Pierce School, especially in the summer when Madrigal cooks. Alas, she tries ...

"I'll be there, thanks!" Walter answered.

"Wonderful! Well, I'd better get back to work." She turned her green-sequined-clad figure and descended back down the staircase to her bookshop. She looked back over her shoulder and said, "You look wonderful in that outfit, Milady! And so much easier to move around without a heavy corset, don't you think?" She disappeared.

They all stared at the vacant spot where the force of nature once stood. Aunt Portia had learned the secrets of the attic when Captain Ahab crossed over.

"I like her!" said Milady suddenly.

Everybody's head turned so quickly to gape at her, she said, "What's wrong? I do!"

Linus wasn't surprised. Portia Easterday had that kind of

magic about her. He made a mental note to remember that. It might come in handy.

Ophelia batted away the thought that maybe the countess was like she was because nobody had ever really, truly been kind to her. Ever.

*Foolishness? Hmm. I suppose you shall have to wait and see.*

*Do people change that drastically?*

*That's a question best answered on a case-by-case basis.*

## twelve

# A Summer Breeze, a Flushing Toilet, and a Master Plan

They stepped out onto the sidewalk just as a truck roared by. Milady screamed and grabbed onto Ophelia's arm. "What was that ... that *thing*?"

"A truck."

She pointed to all the black telephone and power cables we don't see anymore, strung from pole to pole. "And that black rope? Why is it there?"

"It's for electricity," said Linus.

She pointed to the string of cars parked along the edge of the street. "And those are trucks as well?"

"Cars," said Linus. "Short for carriages."

"Oh." She breathed a sigh of relief. "So horses pull them?"

"No. Look, here comes one down the street."

Milady gasped and jumped back three feet. "Oh goodness! Oh dear!" She turned to Ophelia. "So what you were saying earlier? It's all true!"

"Yes."

The countess sat down on the bookshop steps to catch her breath.

Now, I'm just guessing here, but I imagine the Countess

de Winter was truly at a loss for the first time in many, many years. The boys looked at each other, then at Ophelia. She smiled, not a pleasant smile, but an "I told you so" grin.

She sat next to Milady and put her arm around her. "So you see now?"

"Yes. Although it's still quite unbelievable."

"What you need to know is this. We really don't want to hurt you. We want you to get safely back through that circle the day after tomorrow."

"I feel like I have no choice but to believe you," she said.

"I know you won't do this, Milady. But believe me when I say, you can trust us. All three of us."

Across the street in the park, Milady laughed as the breeze hit her skin and swirled the skirts around her legs. "My, my! It's magnificent! I *like* this era."

"Don't get too used to it," said Ophelia.

"Oh, that." She sidled up to Linus and tucked her arm through his. "You can figure out how to let me stay, can't you? You're so smart."

"I could try."

"Linus!" cried Ophelia.

Milady shrugged. "Well, why not? This is a wonderful place. These cars. The lights."

"Things are different now, Milady." Walter stepped beside her on the pathway leading through the park and down to the Bard River. "You'd have to find a place to live, which means you have to pay for it, which means you'd have to find a job."

Her blue eyes clouded with confusion. "A job? Whatever do you mean?"

"Women and men work every day now, Milady." Ophelia

sat down on a park bench and patted the seat next to her. "We don't have to rely on men for our well-being anymore."

Milady sat down. "Really, now? You don't have to marry someone you don't love and"—she screwed up her face—"well, never mind. You don't have to rely on your wits to survive?"

"You do. Just not in the same way. For example, my mother is a scientist. She studies butterflies with my father."

"So she helps him?"

"They work together, fair and square, fifty-fifty."

"How curious." Milady looked out over the river. "Where does the king live?"

"We don't have a king. We don't have lords and ladies and counts and countesses. Our country is founded on the belief that all men are created equal."

Well done, Ophelia!

Milady gasped in horror. "No nobility?"

"Not a one," said Walter. "We still have them in England."

"Walter!" Ophelia hissed.

"I thought we were in England," said Milady.

Ophelia tried to explain the United States of America and democracy in under five minutes.

"Oh, well!" breezed Milady. "As long as women are still pretty and men are still strong and handsome—"

"Want an update?" interrupted Linus, cursing the "an."

Ophelia nodded. "On Madge," she said to Milady.

"Walt?" Linus asked.

The boys sat on the grass.

"Of course, mate. Here it is as I see it," said Walter, leaning back on his hands. "I heard Madrigal and Johann talking over breakfast. He's bringing a lawyer over later today. Anyhow, Madge pleaded with Johann—"

"Pleaded?" Ophelia's mouth dropped open. "Madge?"

The countess's eyes sparkled. An intrigue! How exciting!

"As much as her type does," Walter said, waving to a group of kids from the summer camp next door as they canoed down the river. "Oy!"

They waved back with gusto and shouted like banshees. Linus reminded himself to get back to the camp and finish building the ramp leading down to the yard. The wheelchair-bound children had to go out the front door and around. This would make it easier for everyone.

He's quite handy with hammer and nail.

"He has a right to it, unfortunately," said Ophelia.

"You're right, Ophelia." Walter stood up. "We can only hope he'll have some compassion on his sister." He dropped for a set of push-ups.

"Poor Madge," said Linus.

None of them ever thought they'd say those words. I'll bet you didn't either.

"So let me understand this," said Milady. "This school ...?"

Linus pointed across the street. "Right there."

"This Madrigal. Her brother is trying to take the school away from her?"

Ophelia explained the situation further.

A fire lit in Milady's eyes. "Well, what are we going to do about it?"

"We don't know." Walter looked mournful. "If it closes down, I have to return to London." Walter sat back down. He has trouble remaining still.

Milady pretended to spit. "Pah! I hate that city!"

*Oh good*, thought Ophelia. *Maybe that will upset Walter.*

"So do I," said Walter. "I don't want to go back. Kingscross has quickly become home for me."

*The home place for unintentional orphans*, thought Linus. *Incredible.*

*So much for that*, thought Ophelia. She looked at her watch. "Eleven a.m. We need to go see how Father Lou is faring with d'Artagnan. Maybe he's come up with a way to scare Johann away."

Linus jumped. "Let's go!"

"What is it?" asked Ophelia.

"I've got it!" he said.

The group of four hurried across the park, by the church, and rushed up to the rectory. Milady, if anyone had looked at her, seemed to have come to life. This was drama. This was intrigue. And she'd come along just in time. In all honesty, she didn't really care one way or the other about the outcome just then. She had two days left here in this odd place, and she was going to have a wonderful time!

The group shuffled into the rectory and Father Lou led them into the small living room. Yes, Milady even had an effect on him. Clearly the kitchen wasn't good enough for her like it was for everybody else.

"Have a seat everyone," he said, after the introductions. "D'Artagnan!" he called up the steps.

The toilet flushed.

"He's been flushing the toilet all morning."

"It's magnificent!" said Milady, gently lowering herself in an overstuffed armchair. "As is this chair!"

D'Artagnan trotted down the steps dressed in a pair of

Father Lou's jeans and a Harley Davidson T-shirt. He took one look at Milady and gasped. "Milady! Your clothes!"

"Oh, calm yourself, young man! It's all the mode here."

"Okay!" said Father Lou with a nervous laugh. "Now Linus, you said you have a plan?"

D'Artagnan took a seat in a bent wood rocker.

"Yes, sir." Linus swallowed. He was going to have to speak in whole sentences. Many of them. His heart started to race and his face blushed to a bright magenta.

"It's okay, Linus." Ophelia squeezed his hand from where she sat next to him on the wine colored sofa. "You can do it."

"All right." He inhaled deeply. "We're all aware of the plight of Ms. Pierce. We have to get her brother out of the way."

"I shall challenge him to a duel!" cried d'Artagnan, leaping to his feet and reaching for a sword that was still by the kitchen door.

"Oh, do sit down!" Milady snapped. "Let the boy have his say."

Walter looked from one traveler to the other. These two sure would make things interesting. "Go ahead, Linus," he said.

"Well ..." he cleared his throat. "Umm ..."

"Just say it, son." Father Lou looked as earnest as a priest could be, and that's quite earnest if you ask me.

"Haunted house!" he blurted.

Ophelia's eyes grew to saucers. "You mean *literally* scare Johann away?"

"Uh-huh."

"Brilliant!" Walter cried.

"Inspired!" said Father Lou.

"Magnificent!" D'Artagnan looked ready to start planning right away.

Milady cleared her throat. All eyes turned her way. Her face gave no clue as to what she thought. She stood to her feet, spread her arms, and gave a curtsey. "Meet 'the Gray Lady' of The Pierce School." They cheered. Even d'Artagnan. He arose from his seat and knelt down in front of the countess. He took her hand. "Milady, a truce?"

"For now, young man." Her haughty expression came back full force.

"Ah, for now." His smile was so charming Ophelia almost fell over in her seat.

"Then let's get started," said Father Lou.

"I'll fill Madge in," said Ophelia. "But first, let me show you the costume room, Milady. I'm sure you'll find everything you need there to be the perfect ghost."

"To the garage, men!" Father Lou pointed toward the door.

"We'll be back soon," Ophelia promised. "We can't let you guys have all the fun."

## thirteen

# You Know It's Bad When Madrigal Pierce Will Stoop to a Plan That Might Actually Be Fun

Madrigal Pierce, dressed in a brown skirt that fell almost to her ankles, brown high-heeled sandals, a yellow blouse, and her usual white summer shawl, looked so relieved when Ophelia walked into the parlor of the school, Ophelia almost thought it wasn't Madrigal at all.

The Pierce School for Young People is housed in the old family home, as you know, but when I say "home" what I mean is mansion, and not the houses that pass for mansions these days. This house had twenty bedrooms, now dormitory rooms, and a swimming pool in the basement (still there; Clarice uses it). Senators and geniuses — Einstein himself! — made their way through the beautiful old home. Some people would call it "gracious," a word used frequently to describe stunning homes that were built with good taste. In other words, there isn't frou-frou, curlicues, naked babies with wings, or woodwork so heavy even the Cyclops himself would fail to lift it. *Ask your language arts teacher about the Cyclops. Or your mom or dad.*

Unfortunately, the Pierces seemed to have a genetic predisposition (they were born that way) for dark and gloomy colors. Ophelia looked around in delight. Dark drapes, dark wood, dark walls. Dark, dark, dark.

Excellent!

"Ophelia!" Ms. Pierce cried from her perch on the edge of a blood-red silk settee. *(A settee is a small sofa, sometimes called a love seat, but what is to love about a sofa one can't stretch out on to read?)* "Come in, come in!"

They entered the room Madrigal and Johann's grandmother had decorated back in the thirties. Deep maroons and purples prevailed, mahogany wood still glistened, polished every week without fail.

"I'd like you to meet my brother, Johann." She gestured toward her brother. "Johann, this is Miss Ophelia Easterday."

"Pleasure to meet you, sir." Ophelia put out her hand.

He stood to his feet, a taller, male version of his sister. "Hello." He ignored her hand.

She stuffed it in her pocket.

Johann turned to his sister, his mouth turned down at the corners. "My lawyer should be here in five minutes, Maddie."

Maddie? How nice!

"I need to have a word with you, Ms. Pierce. It shouldn't take but a minute."

"Let's go to my office."

Johann looked about as pleased at this development as a mother whose child has dialed 9-1-1 for the fun of it.

Ophelia had never been in Madrigal's office. It was nothing like the rest of the house. The walls glistened white and shining in the sunlight streaming through a large bay window, the seat supporting two large cream-colored pillows.

Modern, sleek furniture sat on a blond wood floor and all the walls held colorful abstracts. "Oh my!" she said. "This is beautiful!"

"You like this?"

"I love it! Are you kidding me? It's so different—"

"From everything else around here, including me," Madrigal interrupted. "Yes, I know. Have a seat."

Ophelia sat in one of the two pale yellow chairs that vaguely reminded her of a swan that sat in front of Madrigal's desk, a thick glass affair perched on sleek wooden pillars.

Madrigal sat in the other chair. "What is it? You look like you're about to burst."

"I think we've come up with a way to save the school!"

"How did you—"

"Ms. Pierce, the walls have ears in places like this."

"True," she said. "So you all know."

"We can't let The Pierce School close down!" Ophelia realized at that moment how much she actually cared. I mean, she thought she cared before. But sitting in front of the headmistress in her office, and seeing a little bit more of who she really was, Ophelia knew there could be so much more for this woman.

"Maybe it's time. First the fire, now Johann." She paused. "Why do you care?" Madrigal snipped.

"We're friends with Walter and Clarice."

"Oh. Of course." Her mouth turned down.

Ophelia decided to take a chance. Maybe, like Milady, Madge just hadn't been planted in loving grounds in which to flourish. "You're our neighbor, Ms. Pierce. Neighbors help each other out. We just do."

"Not many people feel that way anymore."

"No. But we do!" Ophelia put her hand on the woman's arm. Madrigal snatched it away and glared at her.

*Oh*, she thought. *I guess that was going too far.* "Anyway," said Ophelia. "Let me tell you our idea."

Ophelia was still talking a minute later when Johann banged at the door. "He's here, Maddie. Get to the sitting room!"

"Oh, can it, Joe!" she yelled back. She cleared her throat and Ophelia continued.

"It can't hurt, Ms. Pierce."

"No. It can't. I guess I'd better get in there. But at least I feel a little bit of hope, even though that hope stands upon making this place into a haunted house. It makes me wonder whether to laugh or cry." She sighed. "Thank you, Ophelia."

"We'll be over later on with the basic plans."

## fourteen

# Spit Solves a Multitude of Problems, but Only If it Doesn't Gross You Out

Ophelia went back home to fetch Milady. She had no doubt the wicked countess would find the perfect outfit for scaring the shoes, socks, and black silk shirt off of Johann Pierce.

When she opened the door to the costume room, she almost jumped to the ceiling. There sat the most gruesome-looking woman she'd ever seen who wasn't sporting blood. "Whoa!"

Milady stopped, looking like a well-dressed cadaver (corpse, dead body) sitting in a chair, and jumped to her feet. "You think this is good, then."

"Absolutely!" Ophelia was soundly impressed.

Milady had located a gray dress from the turn of the century (the eighteen-hundreds to the nineteen-hundreds, that is). The gauzy fabric flowed to her feet but there was no train to get in her way. She had taken her stiletto (that sharp little knife with which she earlier threatened Ophelia) to the hem of the skirt and sleeves and tattered them to strings.

"How did you make your face so pale?"

"Your aunt helped me. She helped me with all of this. Oh my, she's a gem, Ophelia, a jewel, a magnificent—"

"Yes, she is."

"And I'm going to frighten that man so much, he'll be running his sorry person back to whatever hole he crawled out of."

"Milady!" Ophelia couldn't help but laugh. "That wasn't very nice!"

"Whatever made you think I was nice, Ophelia?"

Ophelia realized she was having a grand time with this visitor from the enchanted circle. Who would have thought this villainess would be the most cooperative guest yet?

"Let's get back over to the rectory and see what's going on," said Ophelia.

Up in the attic Walter executed his customary push-ups while Linus thumbed through some of the larger, more ancient tomes. Of course he had no idea what was written down, since the book was made up of characters that appeared more like runes than letters of an alphabet. Thankfully, Cato Grubbs left handwritten notes on scraps of paper translating the formulas and ingredients. Some actually described the process as well as the results.

"Look," said Linus. He took a mortar (a stone bowl) from one of the upper shelves, as well as a pestle (a special stone stick used for grinding herbs and other ingredients in the mortar), and set them on the worktable in front of him.

"What are you doing?" asked Walter.

"Hold on," Linus murmured. He rummaged through a brass spittoon (a receptacle made for spitting into) that was filled with plastic baggies with various labels. Some labels were written by a dot-matrix (old) computer printer, others in Cato's hand. Apparently Cato had kept up with technology before he deserted the building twenty years before. Linus chose two bags, one labeled " 'dust to dust' dust," and the other "greener grass from the other side of the fence." He prepared his mind for the experiment. It always helped to be focused, to go through the steps mentally at least three times before actually doing the experiment.

He arranged everything. "All right. I'm going to take two parts grass to one part dust, grind to the finest powder, then spit into the mortar three times. Thank goodness I'm a guy. It has to be guy spit," Linus told Walter.

"It has to be guy spit?" Walter asked.

Linus ignored the question. "After adding the sputum (a more proper yet somehow more disgusting term for spit), I'm going to stir with the spiny end of an egret quill."

There was something to the DNA of an egret. Linus had no idea what it was, and at that point he wouldn't search for the answer. He just wanted to make the experiment work.

A few minutes later he had completed those very steps to perfection.

"What's next?" Walter stood behind Linus's shoulder looking over at the equipment.

"Set it over a flame and simmer until the paste hardens into what should be the size of a dime."

For some reason, Linus didn't mind talking out loud to Walter, especially at his worktable. As the summer progressed, it became more and more like talking to himself.

He followed the instructions to the letter, the process taking about fifteen minutes, giving Walter time to make them PB&Js for a late afternoon snack.

Walter met Ophelia in the kitchen.

"Well." She rooted through the refrigerator for some leftover roast beef from a few days ago. Aunt Portia made a brown meal that also included French onion soup, gravy, and wild rice with mushrooms and pecans. "Milady is getting hungry preparing for her first haunting. I think she might take a nap too."

"I was going to make some PB&Js," he said, hoping Ophelia would take the hint and make him and Linus sandwiches too.

"Help yourself, Walt."

*Blast. Oh well.* He reached for the bag. "Linus is working on an experiment. Fingers crossed."

"Where's d'Artagnan?" she asked.

"He's helping Father Lou fix his motorcycle. Why would that be so fascinating to a musketeer?"

Ophelia started to laugh. "I know exactly why!"

Walter opened the lid to the jar of peanut butter. "And?"

"At the beginning of *The Three Musketeers* he gets made fun of by the Count de Rochefort for having such an old, sorry-looking yellow horse. He got in a fight and didn't end up on the winning end. I bet he's thinking a motorcycle is a much better way to get around."

"Makes sense."

Ophelia and Milady ate their sandwiches and looked on the computer at some fashion blogs. Milady was delighted at the fashions of the day. You can imagine, if she had been able to stay, what a trendsetter the Frenchwoman would have been.

## fifteen

# Never Underestimate the Power of Jewelry

### *or* One Ring to Rule Them All and a Diamond Brooch Can Cause a Lot of Trouble

Ophelia threw her length down on the blue sofa. "Any discoveries?"

"I think so." He opened a copy of *The Lord of the Rings*. "Watch."

Ophelia's eyes rounded in horror. "That book? I hope you know what you're doing, Linus, because I can think of a thousand things that could go wrong."

He shrugged. "I'm just going after the ring."

"Oh, that makes me feel better." She rolled her eyes.

For the past month he'd been trying to find a way to bring artifacts from Book World over to Real World. If characters could travel, why not things? Cato Grubbs did it all the time. So far, however, Linus had experienced a string of failures. He tried bringing the famous wardrobe through, but only a robe covered in bumps appeared. After that, there was the gold straw from Rumplestiltskin debacle. He decided this time he would get it exactly right. He'd measured perfectly, and there in his palm was the pebble he'd created earlier.

He opened up *The Lord of the Rings* and placed the pebble precisely on the word *ring*, making sure it wasn't some other ring. If he was going to get a ring, he wanted the fancy gold one with elvish writing.

Placing the pairing in the middle of the circle, he dropped an eyedropper full of the rainbow liquid onto the pebble precisely at 7:11 and stood back. "We'll see."

Ophelia held her breath. The book glowed as if someone shone ten flashlights from deep in its pages. And as if some unseen hands grabbed the volume, it jumped up, snapped shut, and landed with a thud onto the floorboards. *Much too loud of a thud for a cheap paperback from the bookstore at the mall, I might add. Nobody values quality literature these days.*

Linus picked it up without hesitation while Ophelia shielded the left side of her face as she looked on, wincing.

He opened the book, the pages flipping open to reveal the ring. The. Ring. The ring, ring. Linus gasped. So did Ophelia.

"It's beautiful!" she said, reaching out, eyes glazing over at the sight.

He snapped the book shut, almost on her finger. "No way, Golem."

"Just let me touch it. Just once."

"Nope. Never."

"But—"

"Go downstairs."

"Oh, come on, Linus!"

"Now, Ophelia!"

Ophelia started (jumped a little bit, like when someone sneaks up behind you and pokes you in the side). Linus had never talked to her like that before.

She ran from the room.

*Am I Sam or Golem?* Linus wondered, picking up the

ring. He held it between finger and thumb and examined the play of light on its golden surface. He closed his eyes trying to feel something. Some pull. Anything that seemed to be dangling an obsession at the other end of it.

He waited for three seconds.

Looked again.

Waited for another three.

Really? This was the item that took three long books to dispose of? This was the big deal?

He waited some more.

*Come on! I should feel a little something, right? Didn't Sam?*

He'd always liked Sam. Sam was his favorite character. If he had to be a hobbit, he'd definitely be Sam.

*I, Bartholomew Inkster, prefer to be an elf but that is neither here nor there. And I must ask, does anybody want to be a dwarf? Nobody that I know of.*

Two more seconds. He sighed.

Nothing.

*Good. That's a relief.*

*This little thing might come in handy someday*, he thought, hiding the mystical circle of gold in a jar of monkey bones.


Ophelia lied down on her bed and cried and cried, her voice breaking on each sob like a fog horn. *Don't blame me for the description! I'm just writing down what she told me. I told her that sounded a little harsh but Linus assured me she was spot on.*

Linus had never spoken to her like that. So who was the

one affected by the ring? she wondered. Oh, but it was so beautiful. She thought the words "my precious" and giggled.

*Best to leave it alone.*

But if he could bring the ring over from Book World, what else could he summon over? The notes from Cato Grubbs were clear. The formula only worked on inanimate objects.

Which made her think of Milady and the priceless diamond brooch (pin) that caused quite the hubbub. You see the queen of France had given Lord Buckingham a portion of the pin given to her by her husband. (One has to wonder a bit about the intelligence of French royalty during this time, but it certainly makes for a better story for the heads that wear the crown to be emptier than they should.) Under Cardinal Richelieu's suggestion, the king asked for his queen to wear the brooch at an upcoming ball. Of course, the cardinal was well aware of the queen's gift.

Guess who went to England to retrieve the missing portion?

D'Artagnan!

Guess who went to England to make sure d'Artagnan didn't get the piece back to France?

The Countess de Winter.

Guess who ended up with the missing piece?

Let's just say it wasn't any wonder d'Artagnan wasn't too happy to see the woman who bested him.

*I wonder if we could bring over that pin?* she thought, realizing right away that would make them no better than Cato Grubbs who looted and pillaged Book World on a regular basis. Thinking of Cato Grubbs, why was he mysteriously staying away? What was the mad scientist up to?

Ophelia could only guess. She found Linus.

"I'm sorry," he said.

"Me too."

"I was thinking." He put the last jar, made of a ruby colored stone, on the shelf. "What happens to Milady?"

"Let's just say, her fate is rather drastic, Linus."

He turned quickly toward his sister. "Why in the world do you have to choose people that find themselves in a matter of life and death?"

"It seems as if this time, she chose us." She shrugged. "But you have to admit, it makes it a lot more interesting."

He grinned. She grinned.

He put his arms around his sister and they embraced as they did when they were babies in the same crib.

Everything was once again as it should be.

*Stupid ring*, the twins thought exactly at the same time.

"All right," said Father Lou. "Tonight, stage one, should be easy. Milady should have no trouble. Tomorrow night may not be so easy. Linus? Are you sure you know all that about pulleys?"

"Yes, Father." He didn't mean to sound proud, but Linus fully realized what he did and didn't understand, and pulleys fit into the former category.

"D'Artagnan, are you positive you can swing out from the balustrade at the top of the staircase?"

D'Artagnan took a swig from a can of cold Coke. Linus had never seen a character acclimate so quickly, but then, he seemed to do the same thing in the novel, according to Ophelia.

"Yes. The playacting will be the greater challenge, Father. But Milady will have the bulk of it, and she is quite good at pretending to be something she is not."

*Here we go again*, thought Linus.

"All right," said Walter. "We'll have Madge get Johann out of the house tomorrow evening so we can set up. I'll do backup on that if he won't go with her."

"Good." Father Lou said, and wiped his greasy hands on a rag. "We'll meet at the school around seven and pray everything goes as it should."

## sixteen

# Motorcycle Repair and the Art of Haunting Houses

ℋow much longer do we have to wait?" Milady hissed. "This costume is hotter than a blacksmith's shop."

"We can't do anything until he decides to go to bed," whispered Walter.

"Are you sure I can crawl through the passageway in this get up?"

"It doesn't matter. All you really have to do is get inside. Just to disappear for a bit."

The brother and sister Pierce entered the front door. Johann apparently wasn't up for Madrigal's cooking and Walter couldn't blame him.

"Well, I'm heading off to bed," Madrigal chimed and most unnaturally, I might add.

Walter winced. *Come on, Madge. Keep it cool.*

"I'm going back out then," he said. "I've got things to do."

*What things?* Walter thought.

Madrigal hurried back to her quarters, high heels clicking as usual on the marble floor.

As soon as he heard the door shut, Walter, now out of sight, let the bottom of a heavy chain drop to the floor. The Countess de Winter began to moan.

*Well done!* thought Walter. *You sound like you've been in pain for centuries.*

"Aaaaah-uuuuuuugh. Oh, my looooooooooove."

She winked at him. And moaned some more. Oh, goodness, the woman sounded like all the sorrows of the world had collected in her soul. What an actress Milady was turning out to be.

"What's that?" Johann called. "Who's there?"

"You're on, Milady." Walter whispered and rustled the chain some more.

She turned the corner of the hallway and gliding smoothly without looking to the left or to the right, Milady passed through the gallery, right in front of the rail. She looked almost as if she were on roller skates. She stopped in the middle and looked straight at Johann, her eyes piercing his, then without a sound, continued straight down the hallway to the supply closet where Ophelia would be waiting to help her inside the passage.

Walter ran without sound back to his room.

"Who's there?" Johann shouted. He ran up the steps. When he got to the top ... nothing.

"What's going on?"

Walter was hoping he'd spy the light coming out from under his door.

A knock resounded. *Yes!*

"Come in," he said, crossing one leg over the other, jamming his earbuds in his ears, and picking up his copy of *The Three Musketeers.*

Johann opened the door. "Did you hear anything?"

Walter took out the earbuds. "Other than The Kooks, only you."

Johann leaned against the doorjamb. "Funny, I thought I heard someone moaning...well, never mind. Good evening, then."

"Thank you, sir."

"Yes, well, I'm heading back out, then."

"Oh? Where?"

He shook his head. "This is such a boring town."

*Not if you have the right friends.* Walter laid his book on his chest. "You think?"

"I grew up here and couldn't wait to leave."

"That bad?"

"You could say that. I don't know why Maddie feels so compelled to keep this place going. Then again, she was always sucking up to my father." His mouth turned down in disgust. "Anyway, good night."

"Good night, Mr. Pierce."

When he was sure it was all clear, Walter hurried over to the bookshop, a celebration was in full swing downstairs. Aunt Portia and Uncle Augustus were dancing the jitterbug to the sounds of Glen Miller playing on the hi-fi (record player) in the living room. D'Artagnan was drinking another Coke and trying to get everybody to toast and sing old drinking songs. Father Lou sat in a chair just enjoying the moment.

Linus and Ophelia were slicing a pan of brownies the priest brought over.

And the guest of honor? The Gray Lady herself.

Even beneath the heavy powder, anybody could see that Milady was pleased with herself. In a good way. "My heart was beating so quickly! I just kept thinking, 'Keep calm. Keep calm.' And I did!"

"It was fantastic!" Walter said. "You should have seen

her, everyone. If there's ever been a better impersonation of a ghostly lady, I have no idea where it would have happened, because Milady was brilliant."

"It's always good to have a person of the theatre around," said Uncle Augustus, bringing his sister to a halt.

Obviously, Aunt Portia had been running interference as to why the Countess de Winter was staying in their home. "Indeed!" she said, then stepped to for another round of the jitterbug.

Later that night as Milady was slipping into bed in the guest room, she said to Ophelia. "You know, it's just as exciting to do this sort of thing for the right reason."

"It's true."

Her blue eyes rounded and she smiled. "I never would have thought as much."

Milady picked up her copy of *The Three Musketeers*. She opened the book. "Can you close that window?"

Ophelia's eyes rounded. "Why? It's so hot as it is!"

"I'll get sick and die!"

Ophelia remembered that back in Milady's day, people thought fogs and mists held sicknesses. Bad humors they called them in the days when leeches were a cure and not a problem. Moving well along!

Ophelia smiled. "You won't get sick. Our physicians have proven that you can't get sick from a fog. It's something called a virus now."

Milady screwed up her face. "After your explanation of the America States United, I'll be happy to take your word for it. Fine, then. Leave the window open. Goodnight, Ophelia."

"Have a good sleep, Milady." Ophelia grabbed the doorknob.

"Indeed, I will, and you do the same."

I have a feeling it was one of the best sleeps the Countess de Winter had in years.

D'Artagnan, despite his propensity to fix motorcycles and drink Coke in Real World, is the main protagonist of *The Three Musketeers*. That means the book is mostly about him, and he is what is known in movies as the good guy. The strange thing about this fact is that D'Artagnan is not one of the three musketeers for whom the book is named.

Stranger things have happened, I suppose. *Like the fact that my colleagues in the English department give me no respect, even though, most likely, I've read ten times the amount of books they have.*

I'll do my best here to summarize what Ophelia told Walter as they sat on the banks of the Bard River, the moon sailing in the skies over Kingscross. The same river that was swollen and angry during the flash flood two months before, now almost creaked along like an elderly gentleman who refuses to use a cane. Drought conditions threatened the area with no forecast of rain in sight. The weather had become as heated as d'Artagnan's temperament. The young man from the country would pick a fight if a man so much as looked at him cross-eyed, or not cross-eyed. Just look at him and he might draw his sword.

His great aim in life was to be a musketeer, a special regiment that was assigned to the king himself. So you can imagine the musketeers claimed to be no friend of Cardinal Richelieu! Upon his arrival in Paris, young d'Artagnan managed to insult three of the musketeers, Porthos, Athos, and Aramis, on the first day. But his winning ways and handsome countenance, and not the least of all, his willingness to fight at their side when needed, soon won them over.

But let me tell you a little secret about d'Artagnan. He's much too romantic for his own good. His troubles might have been well more than halved had he not been wont to fall in love at the drop of a hat. (So quickly. And never mind it's a cliché.) He had fallen in love with one of the queen's lady's maids and was set to fall in love with Milady later on. Give that young man an excuse to fall in love and he'd take it with both hands and wish he had a third so he could grab even more!

In short, he was a man who was ultimately filled with desire for two things: to be a musketeer and to love women. His fighter's spirit stood him in good stead for both priorities.

"It's too bad we can't make him fall for Milady sooner than he does in the book," said Walter, who'd bought them popsicles from the corner store nearby when they couldn't stand the heat a moment longer. He sucked the last bit of cherry ice from the stick.

Ophelia did her best to keep the sticky syrup from running down her hand, which meant eating the icy treat faster than usual and getting one of those blinding headaches right behind the bridge of her nose. You wouldn't have known it, though, the way she soldiered through it. "But *really* in love."

Walter twisted the wrapper around the popsicle stick. "Can you think up a reason why he would? Surely there must be something."

"The Countess de Winter certainly is a lot nicer now."

"Isn't she married?"

"The book doesn't really mention a current husband. It

would be a more proper relationship for d'Artagnan, despite the fact that the lady's maid is married to a real jerk."

"Well, maybe we can work on that," said Walter.

Ophelia raised her left eyebrow. "I'm game. And we have most of the day tomorrow to get them together." She grinned. "It's late. Let's get back to the attic."

Walter took her hand again. And Ophelia grinned again, even more widely than before.

"Where has Cato Grubbs been?" Ophelia sat in the backyard at the picnic table with Linus. Walter had already gone over to the school and was probably asleep by now. A midnight moon shone in the sky so brightly it illumined the tabletop Linus had painted a bright red the week before.

"No idea."

"You don't think he's going to throw a monkey wrench into everything, do you?" Ophelia gazed up at Orion's Belt. She loved the stars.

"I wouldn't be surprised."

She sighed. "We need to find out what he's up to. Wait a minute! The brooch!"

"What about it?"

"Can you get it?"

"I don't think so. Not with the portal already opened." Cato's notes had been pretty clear on that.

"If Milady and d'Artagnan found themselves with that much money, they could start a life together. You know as well as I do that Cato is in Book World right now finding that thing. He has to be!"

"You're right."

"Do you think he'd give it up, for a good cause?"

Linus sighed. "I dunno, Ophelia. That's an awful lot of money."

"Can you try to contact him? Please?"

She looked so earnest, he wouldn't have refused her for the world.

"I don't want Milady to die!" she cried. "I like her, Linus. I really do."

"Me too."

Oh my! This was love and greed. This was life and death. Sounds like a novel, does it not?

Ten minutes later, Linus pored over as many books as possible. None had a formula for contacting Cato Grubbs. He looked through leather-covered tomes (large books with many, many words, too many words, if you ask me), paperbacks, even a few scrolls.

"Nothing," he muttered.

An idea hit him. "No way!" he said to no one, his own voice shocking him. He had never talked to himself before.

He hurried down two flights of steps into Aunt Portia's office at the bookstore. He picked up the biggest book of all.

The thick yellow business directory made a nice thump as he dropped it on the desk blotter. He opened it to G.

"Grubbs, Grubbs." He ran his forefinger down the row of names, addresses, and numbers. "No way!"

There it was. Cato Grubbs. Hidden right there in the phone book.

*The man is pure genius*, thought Linus. *But not smart enough to trick me.*

Good for you, Linus. Good for you.

Not caring about what time of night it was, and figuring

mad scientists were most likely night owls, he picked up the phone and dialed the number.

"I'm sorry, this number has been disconnected—"

He dropped the receiver down on the phone's cradle.

A little spark jumped up from the line of type containing Cato's information, whirled around like a fairy, then dove straight into the top of Linus's hand.

"Ow!" He grasped his hand and pulled it to his chest.

He thought he heard a chuckle.

*I deserve it*, he thought, remembering that old saying from King Solomon that pride goes before a fall. In other words, act all smug or think that you are "all that" and you're most likely going to end up being very embarrassed.

Trust me on this one. Old King Solomon knew exactly what he was talking about. Ask your parents about it. I'm sure they have plenty of personal stories they'd rather not share that illustrate precisely how true this is!

## seventeen

# Egads! Being Forced to Hand Write a Letter! What Is This World Coming To?

Linus wasn't quite sure what else to do. Cato Grubbs was good at leaving notes, but was he good at receiving them? Well, there was only one way to find out.

He sat down at his worktable in the attic and composed a letter. *In abominable handwriting, I must add. If a crabbed*

*old branch, dried out and brittle could write, it would write just like Linus Easterday.*

Dear Mr. Grubbs,

As you've most likely guessed, we brought someone through the circle, but so far, you've failed to make things more interesting by throwing your usual monkey wrenches in the mix. Where have you been?

We need a favor, and I'm calling it up as a member of the family. Yes, we found out you're a cousin. I didn't know whether to cheer or boo, but nevertheless, we need d'Artagnan and Milady to fall in love in order to save her life when she gets back into Book World. Yes, they're both here. I'll explain later. Ophelia says we need the brooch. I'll explain that later too, in full detail.

I hope to receive a reply in the morning.

Thank you for your consideration in this matter.

Linus Easterday

*Well! The boy isn't as short on written words as he is in spoken words, is he? Perhaps there's hope for him yet as a communicator par excellence (of great ability).*

He went to bed hoping for a good sleep, but resigned to another night tossing and turning in the heat. And can you blame him? Let's hope he remembers to take a shower in the morning.

Linus arose early, around 7:00 a.m. What Ophelia doesn't

know about her brother is that he is an early riser. She is not. And while she is healthy, she is not wealthy and only sometimes wise. Maybe the old adage about early to bed early to rise is true. Ask your mother or father to quote the thing to you if you don't know it.

The reason she doesn't know is because Linus likes the early hours to himself. It's when he thinks the most clearly, when his best ideas come to him.

That morning, however, he charged right up to the attic (forgetting that shower, unfortunately) in hopes of finding a reply from Cato Grubbs.

A cool front had blown in during the night dropping the temperature in the attic down a touch. He looked with anticipation on the worktable and much to his delight, found a note written in even worse handwriting than his own, but thankfully, similar.

Dear Linus,

So you know, eh? Well, the apple doesn't fall far from the tree now, does it? You must know that in some ways I view you as my protégé, hoping that my genius will carry on through you. Not completely, I must add. Nobody can be as wonderful as myself, but you might at least make it halfway.

You guess correctly that I'm back in Book World looking for that blasted diamond pin you requested. This should fetch a pretty penny on the black market. The literary value be cursed, this item will stand up on its own! So forget it!

Of course, you might be able to beat me to it. But

to find out how, you are on your own, and trust me,
Cousin, I wouldn't advise going up against me just
yet. Besides, no one should ever accuse me of making
things easy on you. I couldn't live with myself if I did.
However, to give you at least a sporting chance, look
for a black leather volume with XI in red on the spine.

                    Your second cousin thrice removed,
                                 Cato Julius Grubbs

*Julius?* Linus thought. That was his own middle name!
And Ophelia's was Julia. He wondered why. Did it have something to do with *The Tragedy of Julius Caesar?* It was the
only Shakespeare play he'd ever read and Julius Caesar died.
Who wanted to be named after the victim? He didn't. But
what could a fellow do? It's not like the Drs. Easterday had
given him a choice.

*A brief note here to you, dear ones, about names. If you
have a ridiculous name, my condolences. (I, for one, completely relate. My middle name is so preposterous I've only
uttered it aloud when forced by a real and present threat,
like the IRS and Mrs. Cunningham, my first grade teacher.)
And know that someday, you can change it if you'd like.
Mom and Dad, if you don't like this, don't blame me. I'm not
the one that chose a perfectly awful name for your offspring.*

*Stop thinking about names,* Linus thought, as he began
looking at the books on the shelves and tables. *You don't
have much time.* XI. *(The Roman numerals for eleven, for
any reality TV dullards that somehow found a copy of this
book in their hands.)* He scanned the volumes, trying not

to skim too fast, looking for black bindings. Brown leather bindings, most veined with faint cracks, were the most popular, naturally. Some green spines rested in between them, usually with gold lettering, but several blared red script, one in particular promising a thousand and one uses for talcum powder.

Talcum powder.

Can you think of a more boring book? And have you ever tried to clean up an explosion of talcum powder?

He saw some of the old faithfuls. *Stage Presence, Stage Presents, the Art of Showing Up and Showing Off.* Perfect for a person like Cato. Perfectly horrid for a person like Linus. *Trapdoors to Literary Realms*, Linus's personal favorite.

*He said I'd have to look for it myself. Maybe it's hidden somewhere more obscure*, thought Linus, suddenly feeling the thrill of excitement. In looking for the book he might find some other treasures. The thought quickened his pace.

Walter hated the fact that he was a sneak, but he'd learned from the best, an older lad named Troy, on the streets of London. Still, he wasn't foolish enough not to use his gifts for the greater good. His lock-picking skills came in handy when trying to find Quasimodo, as well as his street-fighting skills when the bullies in the park made fun of the young hunchback and picked a fight with Walter. And hey, the other fellow threw the first punch. Walter was simply trying to avert the blow and send him on his way! His ability to run fast from the scene of a crime stood him in good stead when running through the woods to lure Captain Ahab to the river.

This morning, however, those street senses set off that

familiar alarm in his belly when he awakened. Something wasn't right.

People call this feeling intuition. It's when a person knows something, but they don't know how they know it. Some call it a gut feeling because one quite often feels it in his or her stomach. Some just call it indigestion and go about their day.

Walter, having avoided many a scrape by listening to that little voice, always took heed. It wasn't something he talked about much. He didn't want anyone to know how he came by such a thing. He wanted to leave his life in London behind.

That morning, after eating a breakfast of cold cereal that tasted like bird food, he heard the creak of the garden gate and watched as Johann climbed in and started the engine. Obviously the fellow was an early riser.

*Too bad he isn't as cool as his van,* Walter thought, admiring the old, dark green VW Westfalia.

His inner alarm was blaring like a firetruck, so much so that he pressed a hand to his stomach.

*What grandiose bad thing would a guy like Johann Pierce do?* Nothing came to Walter's mind. The guy was so tall and skinny it seemed as if the slightest breeze would knock him down. And he just didn't seem like the type to really do anything that would take real fortitude. He had that sourness about him that seemed to stem from weakness.

*You're being daft, Walt. Utterly daft.*

Maybe the feeling would go away.

Linus rummaged through Cato's desk drawers, and let me tell you, that is not an easy job. Cato Grubbs is what some people call a pack rat. He cannot throw anything out. Do you want to know why Cato left the lab in the first place? Other

120

than the main reason, which we will get to later, he simply ran out of room and didn't need the enchanted circle any longer to travel from Book World to Real World.

Oh dear, the whole house was quite filled with all manner of paraphernalia (miscellaneous items, usually necessary for a particular activity, in this case, Cato's experiments), from old bicycles to packing peanuts. Engine parts, crates of bottles, a doll collection that no little girl would have wanted. Yes, they were that strange. A crate of Pink Bubble soda and all sorts of brown bottles labeled with names only a scientist would understand.

Portia, after spending a good portion of her life writing books, had decided to start selling them instead. Strangely enough, they found a flyer from a realtor on their front door, extolling the benefits of the shop on Rickshaw Street, with a phenomenal price. Of course they bought it.

And now, here they all were. Linus going through another man's rubbish, Portia downstairs making coffee for Milady, Augustus at the kitchen table tapping his chin with the pen he was using to make a to-do list for the twins, and Ophelia still softly snoring in her bedroom. Most likely her sheets appeared to have been taken up in a giant hand and twisted, her legs and arms poking out.

Nothing resembling a black tome was hidden in the desk. He decided to crawl under the worktable and see what was in the boxes beneath it.

After an hour, he grumbled within, miffed it was taking this long to find the book. Then again, with Cato Grubbs involved, he should have expected as much.

## eighteen

# Just When You Thought People Can Change, Someone Comes Along and Destroys Your Faith in Humanity

Ophelia threw another outfit together from Ronda's offerings and headed into Milady's room. *We have to get started early on d'Artagnan this morning*, she thought.

"All right, Milady! Rise and shine!" she chimed, a surefire way to awaken someone and directly plunk them down headfirst into an awful mood.

However, Milady, like Linus, was a morning person. One never knows about these things. We somehow rarely think of a book's antagonist (bad guy) as a morning person.

She opened her eyes. "Ophelia! Good morning!" she said with a smile.

"I've got clothes for you. I think you'll like the outfit."

She laid out a gypsy skirt in sky blue and another T-shirt, this one in bright white with gold embroidery around the neckline.

Milady clapped. "Beautiful! I love this era. Can we look at clothing on that lighted box again?"

"Sure. Go ahead and get dressed, and I'll bring us some breakfast." Ophelia put her hand on the doorknob to go.

Milady threw back the covers. "Ophelia?"

"Yes, Milady?"

"Do you think people can change?"

*Wow*. Ophelia folded her arms across her chest. "It depends on how badly they want to, I suppose. Or why."

Milady nodded. "That's what I thought. But some circumstances make it easier than others, don't they?"

"I'd agree with that."

"Thank you. You may go." Milady dismissed her.

Ophelia closed the door with a smile.

Twenty minutes later the pair walked across the street, arm in arm like girlfriends. Ophelia still wondered whether or not she had been taken in by the Countess de Winter. But honestly, what did Milady have to gain in any of this?

Absolutely nothing.

She squeezed her arm, Milady squeezed back, and they laughed together as they walked up to Father Lou's kitchen door.

Walter found Linus in the attic, still searching for the book in yet another box of junk. Linus explained his task. "No luck yet, though."

"Sorry, mate." He jammed his hands in his pocket and looked around. "This place is awful and yet fantastic, isn't it?"

Linus couldn't see the awful about it, but he didn't want to argue. That took too many words and he was already tired from all the searching. "Yep."

"Well, point me in some direction, any direction, and I'll have a go as well."

Walter never shirks from lending a helping hand. A true friend. No wonder everyone likes him so much. King Solomon, that wise old sage, once said, "A man who would have friends needs to be friendly himself," or something of that nature. You'd do well to remember that. We all would. The world would be a much nicer place, wouldn't it?

*(How was that, parents? Did it make up for my tirade about terrible names? Good.)*

Linus had always liked his hair. The light blond color made it easy for Ophelia to find him, and it kept his head warm in the winter. Therefore, he had no interest in pulling it out, which is just what he felt like doing.

"We've looked everywhere," he mumbled.

"What do you suggest?" Walter dropped for some push-ups.

"No idea."

"I'll get us a snack."

"Great idea."

Walter headed down to the kitchen.

When Cato Grubbs said he wouldn't make it easy on him, he wasn't kidding. Linus hoped and prayed he wouldn't grow up to be as maddening an adult as his distant cousin.

"Come on!" he cried out in frustration, balling his hands into fists. He fell back down into the chair at his worktable, a very nice leather office chair, by the way. Some people have all the luck. He set his elbows on his knees, dropped his forehead into his hands and ground the heels of his hands against his eyelids.

*Calm yourself, Linus. It's going to be okay. You'll find it.*

He sat in stillness for another minute, then raised his head. A sound in the corner near the blue couch snapped his gaze in that direction. A rustling, almost as if it came from a small animal, scratched at the wall, then stopped.

Linus arose and walked toward the corner, feeling a little

uncertain. I can't blame him, can you? After all that searching he'd done, it might have been anything from just a little field mouse to some odd robotic miniature machine that could shoot lasers straight from its eyes and clear through your body. Oh, I just hate those things, don't you?

But it wasn't either of those things. Instead, a book leaned against the corner, a black book, a large black book. And on its cover? You guessed it. The number eleven in crimson Roman numerals.

Linus grabbed it with both hands and hurried back to his worktable. He breathed in deeply, then opened the book. Here it was. The secret to bringing people through the portals at will. He was surprised Cato was actually willing to dispense such information so quickly. Maybe he was a natural at this! Maybe he was destined to surpass his eccentric second cousin thrice removed!

The pages of the book snapped open to another passage.

*Huh? A television screen? How in the world?*

Static covered the screen like a million black and white ants milling around a square of spilled syrup. *(And would somebody please clean that mess up? I already have enough to do in the English department. Thank you.)*

But the black and the white separated to reveal a man. Cato Grubbs to be precise, and he was laughing so hard he could barely breathe. His light curls bounced with each "Ha!"

Linus sighed. *Great. Just Great.*

Finally, the gales of laughter abated (calmed down) and Cato reached into the breast pocket of his pale green brocade coat, pulled out a white handkerchief and mopped his sweaty, flushed cherubic face. Linus could tell he was dressed in the garb of *The Three Musketeers* time period and actually, he didn't look much different than usual. The man does love his ruffles.

"Don't you want to know what's so funny?" Cato asked, feeding the slip of fabric back into the pocket.

"Can't wait."

"Now, now, Cousin Linus, don't be a spoilsport." He leaned closer to the screen. It was foolish to think there was actually a camera. No, this was a portal to be sure, but only a visual one, Linus surmised. "You actually thought I was going to let you in on the secret, didn't you?"

Linus didn't move. Not one muscle. He didn't even blink his eyes.

Cato laughed again. "No worries, lad. I would have thought the same thing, out of sheer hope more than anything else."

Linus had to nod at that.

"I like your pluck, Linus. You'll go far."

"I have a quick question before we talk about the brooch, Cousin." Linus leaned closer to the book. "Why do you go into Book World to bring back artifacts when clearly there's a formula to bring them through without all that?"

"What have you brought through?"

Linus didn't wish to say.

"You'd best spill it, boy. Trust me."

"The ring from *The Lord of the Rings*."

Cato began laughing again. "From what part of the book?"

"The flashback scene where Golem finds the ring at the bottom of the river."

"Quick! Go get the copy." Linus did while Cato said, "Oh, this will be rich."

Linus grabbed the book off the shelf near the door.

"Open it!" Cato cried from the book-screen.

Linus did. "There's nothing written here."

"Exactly. You have to be careful about these things, lad. And where did you put the ring?"

"In the jar of monkey bones."

"Go ahead and get it."

Linus reached onto the shelf and opened up the jar. Odd. He dug deeper. What? Then ran his fingers along the bottom of the container. "Empty!"

"Precisely. If you call something forward from the attic, it only lasts for a certain period of time, and there's no going back in no matter what copy you use. Effectively, no one else will ever get to see the real ring, Linus. You were it. The only one."

"Other than Ophelia."

Cato waved a hand. "Right. Whatever. Now, the brooch." He looked to his right, then to his left, and said, "Ready?"

"Yes," said Linus.

"Is anything in the circle?" asked Cato.

"Nothing."

"All right. Stand clear. We're transmitting."

Just like it did at 11:11 p.m., the circle glowed and pulsed through the rainbow ending in its crystal white light. The sparks flew and when the smoke cleared, there was nothing.

Cato Grubbs laughed and laughed.

"Do you not get it?" cried Linus. "We need that brooch."

"Why?"

Linus explained.

Cato laughed some more. "Don't *you* get it, boy? True love is strengthened in the fires of adversity. If you three do your job, a priceless brooch should make no difference at all. Now shut the book please, I have work to do. But remember what I said. It's important."

Oh, how rich. Cato Grubbs giving out relationship advice. Would wonders never cease?

## nineteen

# Tragedy Is Never Funny, Unless You Produce a Reality Show That's Been Cancelled, but Other Than That ...

Linus and Walter sat with Father Lou working out a series of pulleys, the first of which would suspend Milady out over the school's entry way, the second which would hold d'Artagnan as he swept in, grabbed her, and pulled her back over the balustrade. Oh, the argument that would then ensue.

"This is going to be brilliant," said Walter. "Absolutely brilliant!"

Linus, as always, felt a little nervous. "I'm still concerned for their safety. We need to test the line for that kind of weight."

"Sounds good to me." Father Lou pulled tight on the line currently attached to d'Artagnan's pulley. "Let's go to the top of the church bell tower and give it a whirl."

Throwing something over the edge of a window high up in a wall. If you can think of anything better for three males, let me know, because I clearly cannot.

Briefly, Ophelia explained her matchmaking scheme to Father Lou while Milady and d'Artagnan went to find out how the pulleys were coming along.

He raised an eyebrow and turned on the oven. "Really, Ophelia? That sort of thing never works out, you know."

"Can it hurt to try, though? I hate to think of Milady going back there and continuing on down her road to ruin."

He laughed. "Road to ruin? You crack me up."

"So she can hang out over here today?"

"Why not? That doesn't seem like too much interference. And he does fall for her later on in the book." He reached into the refrigerator and pulled out a roast and a bag of carrots. "Pot roast tonight. Dinner here?"

"Thanks."

"What are you going to be doing the rest of the day?"

"I have another hundred pages to go in the novel."

"You haven't read it all yet?" He opened the pantry and pulled out some potatoes and a couple of onions.

"No. It'll be fine though."

Brave words, Ophelia. You see, if she doesn't read the rest of the novel by the time the portal opens again, the character is doomed to fizzle to nothing in the acids between the worlds. So far they'd avoided such fates for their visitors.

She realized how cavalier she'd been. "I'd better go."

Rushing up to her room she heard Uncle Augustus calling her. But remembering that list of chores, she pretended not to hear. Oh, you've *never* done that? Please.

Walter made his excuses to the crew at Father Lou's. He still didn't feel right about things. What did his mother call it at times? That's right. A sense of impending doom. He thought of school fires, and pulleys breaking, and characters fizzing painfully away. I mean, what could go wrong? Right?

Still, he needed to sit by himself for just a bit, think

rationally about all that was going on and maybe figure out why he felt like this.

He entered the school from the street and had just ascended the grand staircase when Madrigal let out a cry of frustration and stomped her foot on the floor of the dining room. He stopped, tuning his ear in that direction. Maybe Johann just told her how to properly make tuna salad. He smiled as he remembered his dear mum's food, not much better than Madrigal's.

"Look, Maddie! I don't even know why you want to stay in this spooky place! It's just creepy."

"What do you mean? You grew up here too."

No response.

Madge paused. "You saw her, didn't you?"

"What? No."

"No, who? You know exactly what I mean. You saw the Gray Lady, didn't you?"

"Of course not."

Walter crept back down the steps and stood at the wall next to the dining room entrance.

"You don't want to know who she is? Well, I'll tell you anyway because she wasn't around when we were growing up."

Johann said, "Suit yourself." But Walter heard the interest in his voice.

"Remember that old house across the street and up the block? The Wethington place?"

"Yes. When did they tear that down?"

"Three years ago. She came over here after that. Come, brother, you know you saw her. Admit it."

He still said nothing.

Walter held his breath. Nobody told Madge what the Gray Lady's story was. How would she do? Thankfully she'd been updated about what was happening in the evening. Would she set the groundwork?

"She's one of those ghosts of love lost."

Johann harrumphed. "Figures. We can't even have an extraordinary ghost. Just another pale, blond female pining over being left by a boyfriend who probably didn't much love her to begin with."

*What a sentimental old fool*, Walter thought.

"I thought you didn't see her."

"Nevermind that. You might as well finish the tale."

"The Wethington house has a grand entry like ours with a balcony at the top of the steps."

"Yes, yes. I know." His impatience was beginning to bother Walter. For some reason, he just did not like this man. He felt that in his gut too.

"It's not like you thought. She had a baby while her husband was off fighting in the civil war. It was the wintertime and the child died, the same day she heard that her husband had been killed in battle."

Walter found himself feeling such sorrow. *Hold up, mate. This is just a story.*

Great job, Madge! First a soft spot for d'Artagnan, now this. While Ophelia's matchmaking, she should try to put her together with Father Lou.

Now *that* would be a match made in heaven. (There's that sarcasm again.)

"She threw herself over the balcony that night."

"She sure moaned painfully," said Johann.

"But even worse …"

*Oh, Madge. Don't take it too far!*

"The army was wrong. Her husband wasn't dead!"

"Have you ever seen her, Maddie?"

"No. I just hear her. I feel sorry for her, believe it or not. So what are you going to do, Johann?"

"I'll get you out of here, Maddie. Onc way or another. I promise you."

"You never liked me, did you?" she asked.

"No."

"Why?"

"You killed mother the day you were born. How can anybody forgive that?" he said.

Madrigal went charging through the door, high heels clicking furiously as she ran across the foyer and down the side hallway to hcr office. Walter was up the steps before her door slammed shut.

*We never know the pain people bear inside. How can wc?* Walter's heart broke for Madrigal Pierce.


At 4:30, Ophelia set down the book, feeling more concern for Milady than ever. But what could she do? When she entered Father Lou's manse, the smell of pot roast, even on a summer's day, brought a feeling of homey warmth she recognized but had never really known. *We all know what is true and good instinctively, don't we? I would say pot roast falls into that category with ease. And the fact that walking into a home with the smell of a wonderful meal meeting you at the door was an odd occurrence for Ophelia Easterday makes me sad. Hopefully your parents are better at providing you with such experiences than hers were. And if they are, be thankful. A fine roast beef is nothing to sneeze at, dear ones.*

Father Lou was just cleaning and paring some strawberries. "Making strawberry shortcake for dessert. Everybody's invited. Well, all the haunted house gang, that is."

"Perfect." Her aunt and uncle were headed down a little later to Birdwistell's to play bridge. They were on their own for dinner anyway. "How's the pair?"

"Actually, not too bad. Milady's been sitting in a lawn chair all day reading *The Three Musketeers* and d'Artagnan's been doing a great job on my motorcycle. The guy has a real flair for mechanics."

Ophelia laughed. "You just never know. I thought he would be the most exciting character that's ever come through the circle, and he's been the most boring by far."

He dropped the last strawberry into the bowl and reached for the sugar canister. "Maybe he's realizing that a simple life well-lived isn't such a bad thing after all."

Ophelia held up a set of crossed fingers. "Here's hoping."

Milady walked in and tossed the book on the kitchen table. "I skipped to the end." Her milky skin, obviously whole milk before, had changed to the color of skim milk. Not a pretty sight. "I can't believe it." She turned to Father Lou. "I'm scared to go back now. I don't want to die."

Ophelia grabbed her hand and pulled her down into the chair next to her. "It doesn't have to work like that."

"What do you mean? The book is written! There it is on the page in ink. And ink remains." She hugged herself. "I . . . I don't know what to do. I know if I don't go back, I'll die. And if I do go back, I'll die. Can somebody not find a way to help me?" Tears filled her eyes.

If Ophelia had even one atom of doubt left that the Countess de Winter had not changed, it went spinning off into space never to be seen again. *(All right, I'm no physicist! I realize that. I have no idea if atoms just go spinning off into space willy-nilly. You'll have to ask a scientific person. I'm a man of letters not of science. And if you don't like it, you can very well take it up with the administration, but on this matter, I doubt they'll even give you an audience. Don't say I didn't warn you!)*

Ophelia placed a comforting hand on Milady's arm. "It doesn't work that way."

"What do you mean?" Her gaze shot straight into Ophelia's.

"She means she has good news." Father Lou stirred a hefty amount of sugar into the strawberries.

"It's true. What you do *does* matter, Milady. You can change your future. The words of Dumas aren't written in indelible (permanent) ink."

"Truly?"

"Oh yes! Quasimodo went back to thirteenth century France, and he didn't die like he was supposed to. He ended up living a great life! And last time, with Captain Ahab, same thing! Coming through the enchanted circle made all the difference for them. And it can make all the difference for you."

A tear slipped down her cheek. "But I've done so much. I almost don't know how to go back to those days before ..." She shook her head.

"What happened, Milady? Who steered you in the direction you found yourself?"

This was something Ophelia had been wondering lately. Was there a past to these characters that the author himself did not know? Did they truly come through as complete human beings with a childhood behind them? She was about to find out.

## twenty

# Firm Resolve and a Good Meal, Necessary for Any Proper Haunting

"My childhood is very foggy now," Milady said. "In fact, I don't remember much before my marriage to Athos."

"One of the three musketeers." Ophelia began peeling a piece of corn from the sack Father Lou set down on the table. Well, so much for a past history. "That didn't work out too well, did it?"

She shook her head. "I know stealing the communion chalice was wrong, but he hung me, Ophelia! My own husband hung me *after* I was already branded!"

"You wouldn't even go to jail for something like that nowadays," said Father Lou.

"No!" Milady's hand flew up to her mouth. "And you're a priest! What would you do?"

"Pray for the thief and hope God will have mercy and send what they need in their lives to choose to do the right thing." He shrugged. "I know, that must sound crazy to you."

"No, no, no! It sounds like forgiveness." She dropped her face in her hands. "I'm so sorry. To everybody I've wronged for so long. Even Athos. Maybe he just didn't know any better."

"Who knows?" said Ophelia, picking off the strands of

blond silk stuck to the corn. "But even with all of that, you can choose to go back and be a good person, Milady. In fact, I can put you back in a place where you can simply disappear."

"How will I live?"

Ophelia felt her heart heavy with compassion. "Is there anybody you can trust?"

She shook her head quickly from side to side.

"What about d'Artagnan?" asked Father Lou.

*Nice one, Father*, thought Ophelia.

Milady shrugged. "But he knows all about me. He's been rather nice today, though."

"What if we talk to him? Just ask him to look out for you? To help you carve out a new life?"

"Oooh, I wish I could do it on my own!" Milady slammed a hand down on the table.

"The times are different now," Father Lou said gently. "It's all right. There's nothing wrong with asking for help when you need it, Countess, even if it's from a man. D'Artagnan is brave at heart, and kind. Maybe you two can find a way to exist in harmony together."

She nodded, resolve sparking in her eyes and stiffening the cast of her chin. "I'm going to talk to him. Right now."

"Well, make it quick then, Milady. Dinner's in ten minutes!" He laughed.

She made for the door, then turned back. "You really think I can do this?"

"Yes!" both Ophelia and Father Lou yelled with broad smiles on their faces.

She lifted a fist and shook it. "Wish me luck!" Then disappeared.

Ophelia let out a windy sigh of relief.

"What was that all about?" asked Father Lou.

She picked up another ear of corn and split the tight husks up at the top. "Linus and I were trying to get the brooch over here so she'd have some money to get a fresh start."

"But that brooch doesn't belong to her, Ophelia. Not to sound like a pastor or anything, but, you know."

She laughed. "Oh, please. Go right ahead. I'm glad it didn't work out."

"Some of our worst plans don't. And that's a good thing."

*Truer words never spoken, as somebody once said. Probably that fellow Shakespeare.*

Oh, what a grand meal! The entire gang sat around Father Lou's living room and consumed his good food. The man can nourish the stomach as well as the heart, a wonderful trait in a clergyman.

"Let's drink a toast!" Walter raised his glass of lemonade. "To tonight! To Linus's pulleys, Milady and d'Artagnan's bravery, Father Lou's good food to bolster us up, Ophelia for knowing the story, and of course, to Madge for, unbelievably, going along with it all!"

"We should have invited her," said Father Lou. Linus looked at him like he was crazy. "Why not? She's not so bad."

"And to you, Walter," said Milady. "For having such a kind heart and helping hands."

They clinked their glasses together and drank down the cool drink. The time was 6:00 p.m. Three and a half hours and counting.

"It will be quite a show," said Father Lou.

Unfortunately, he didn't know the half of it. Or maybe that was a good thing.

# twenty-one

# Boo! A Terrible Haunting
## *or* Corsets, Pulleys, and Loads and Loads of Makeup

Ophelia put the final touches on Milady's makeup in Clarice's room. Clarice looked on. "I'm glad you know how to do that stuff," she said.

"I don't. But a ghost is a ghost, right?"

Milady was pale enough on her own. "Are you sure that rope will hold me?"

"I am, Milady."

"It'll be fine!" said Clarice, who insisted in being in on the haunt. "Linus is a genius when it comes to stuff like that."

Girlfriends always think their boyfriends are geniuses. Even if their IQ is no higher than the temperature of a late spring evening. *(That would be around seventy-five or eighty for the dullards out there, of which, you, reader, are clearly not one!)*

"Everything went fine when we practiced. It will hold." Ophelia messed up Milady's hair a little more, then stepped back. "It really says something about you when no matter what I do, you still look beautiful."

Milady reached out a hand and held Ophelia's cheek.

"How old are you?" Ophelia asked.

"I don't know for sure, but I think I'm in my thirties. Well, let's get moving. The head of the school should be coming soon."

They met the others at the balcony, including d'Artagnan who was wearing Walter's party costume, only dusted with white powder. *He* looked frightening. He stood there, sober.

"Can you do this?" Walter asked him. "Are you sure it will be all right?"

"I did it earlier, isn't that right?" He looked at the countess. "You are magnificent."

Linus stepped forward with a carabiner (rock climbing hook). He reached into a hole made in the back of Milady's bodice and grabbed the hook on her harness. The black line went up to a pulley in the ceiling about four feet away from the balustrade. He had a great time with Walter and Father Lou installing it. Another pulley was installed about three feet to the right. They attached the line to a harness beneath d'Artagnan's clothes.

Down in the foyer, Clarice and Ophelia lit the candelabra on the side table, two of them, with eight candles each. They turned off the chandelier to keep as much light off the ceiling as possible.

All waited in silence, their breath coming shallow in their anticipation. All was ready. All had been checked and double-checked. The trial run went smoothly. What could happen?

Five minutes later, Madrigal jammed her key in the lock as loudly as she could. When she pushed open the door, the Gray Lady began to moan. Slowly, she traversed across the balcony.

Both Linus and Ophelia felt the hairs on the back of their neck raise. *Oh, please*, Ophelia thought. *Please let this work!*

Johann looked up and pointed. "There she is!"

"The Gray Lady!" Madrigal pointed too. "My goodness, she's magnificent!"

Milady increased her volume, then stopped in the middle of the balcony. "You!" she pointed a finger at Johann. "Leave this place and never come back!"

She climbed onto the rail with the help of a box that had been placed there. Thank goodness it was even dimmer upstairs than in the foyer. "Aaaaaaaoooooohh!" she cried. "My husband! My child." She let her face fall in her hands, and she wept some more. Then she stood up straight, reached out her arms, and fell forward. She was airborne.

Johann, with an expression of horror, looked as if he was about to faint. But the expression appeared on all their faces as, Milady's weight now stretching the rope, the loud sound of screws displacing from the plaster ceiling let out a pop!

Milady screamed. "Help me! Please!"

"Hang on!" cried Linus coming into view. "Stay calm."

"What's going on?" yelled Johann.

Linus tried to reach for her rope. "Too far."

The rope jerked again as the pulley was further tugged from the ceiling. Another scream from Milady. "Please!"

Ophelia screamed too, grabbing the balcony with tight fingers. "D'Artagnan! Now!"

D'Artagnan jumped up easily on the balcony, his feet balanced and poised, and just as the pulley snapped, he swung forward and snatched the Countess de Winter into his strong arms.

The metal pulley fell to the floor, clattering loudly on the marble.

But the weight of both people would not hold for long. The same popping of screws began. Walter slid down the stair railing, pulled off the cushions on the small settee at the back of the foyer, and just as he arranged them beneath the pair, the pulley gave way, and they came falling down together, landing in a puff of talcum powder.

"Is everybody all right?" Father Lou rushed down the steps.

"I think so," said Milady, even more pale beneath her powder.

"I'm fine." D'Artagnan stood and held a hand out to the countess. She took it and rose to a standing position, her knees shaking, her hands shaking, her head shaking, everything quivering with adrenaline.

She threw her arms around d'Artagnan and began to laugh.

"This is crazy!" Johann came to his senses. He turned to his sister. "Maddie, you are off your rocker! Did you have anything to do with this?"

Linus sucked in his breath. Would she make them take the fall?

*Take the fall. Yes, there's a certain irony to it, isn't there?*

Her eyes blazed, and she turned on him. "Yes! These people are my friends, Johann. That they would go to such lengths to help me, when you, my own brother wish to bring me down to ruin, is a loyalty you would know nothing about. Now get out! Get out of this house."

"It's half mine, Maddie. I'll stay if I like."

Father Lou, bounty hunter and man with a keen sense

of right and wrong, stepped forward. "You might be wise to move along tonight, Mr. Pierce."

"Who are you?" he sneered.

"Don't mess with him." Walter stood beside the priest and crossed his arms over his chest. "He's hurt more people than a man like you could ever dream of."

"You're a bully!" Ophelia, someone who knew a bully when she saw one, stepped forward.

Linus joined the line. Then Clarice. Followed by d'Artagnan and Milady.

Madrigal lifted her chin. "Get out."

"You know you'll have to give this place up. I have the right."

"Get out, now." Madrigal joined the line.

"I'll get my bags," he huffed.

"Uh ... no," said Father Lou softly. "You're just going to go through that door. And we'll make sure you don't step through it again without a lawyer with you."

"This isn't over, Maddie." Johann looked at his sister with such hate, Ophelia wanted to cry. Too bad Madge couldn't remember her childhood like Milady.

Madrigal lifted her chin, the proud headmistress of the school, the wronged sister, and just perhaps, the friend of those gathered in the room for her defense.

Johann stalked out, slamming the door behind him.

"That went well," said Walter, rolling his eyes.

"I am so sorry, Ms. Pierce," said Ophelia.

"Me too." Linus couldn't believe what happened. He felt so defeated. He was so sure everything was safe. "To everybody. I let you down."

Milady hit him on the shoulder with a laugh. "You sure did!"

Madrigal shook his hand and placed the other hand on his shoulder. "You've got nothing to be ashamed of, Linus. Sometimes matters don't work out the way we'd like, but they still work out to the good."

Father Lou agreed. "We're all safe and Johann is out of the house. At least for now. I'd say it's a job well done."

"We'll find a way to get him off your back, Ms. Pierce," Walter promised.

Madrigal nodded, then turned back into her efficient self. "And now, everybody, to bed! We've all had quite the night!"

# twenty-two

# Nothing Worse Than a Genius Feeling Sorry for Himself, Except a Brother Who Can't Take a Hint

### *or* Liar, Liar, Pants on Fire

Ophelia, Linus, and Walter sat around Linus's room. Linus at his desk, Walter on the beanbag chair, Ophelia flat on the bed with her arms out at her side. "It wasn't your fault, Linus," she said.

"Then whose was it, Ophelia?" he said, more angry with himself than he'd ever been. "Really?"

"What I'm trying to say is—"

"I designed it. I installed it. I tested it. And they could have been killed."

Walter sat up straight. "He's right, Ophelia. But here's the thing, mate. Nobody got killed. So thank heaven for that. And tomorrow, we'll go over and examine everything. See where the weaknesses lie. Until then, there's no use in beating yourself up about it. There might be a perfectly reasonable explanation."

"Something you couldn't have known!" said Ophelia.

The guys looked at each other. She just didn't get it. But they loved her all the more for it.

"The last night with this pair." Walter sighed. "This was fun."

"Seems a little anti-climactic, though." Ophelia reached toward the nightstand and slipped off a copy of *Popular Science*. "Do you think they should be back already?"

D'Artagnan and Milady had gone out for a late stroll in the park. She'd been so shaky after the fall, d'Artagnan suggested they get some air.

"Maybe. But the fact that it's taking a long time can only be good."

Ophelia flipped open the magazine. "I don't know how she's going to do it, guys. I honestly don't know how she'll be able to mend her ways."

"Are you joking?" Walter said. "She's the most resourceful person in the entire book. Why should it be any different because she's doing it for the right reason?"

Ophelia agreed on the surface, but deep down, she still had her doubts.

Have you ever woken up, gotten ready for school, and hopped on the bus only to be told by your friends, in the most animated voices of course, about the *huge* storm that passed through? How everybody in their houses lied awake in their beds, the flash of lightening illuminating their faces like a strobe light, the crack of the thunder beating against their eardrums like taiko drums? (Those are the mammoth drums Japanese drummers use, banging them with mallets and creating beats that vibrate your insides.)

That's what would have happened to the twins had it not been summertime. Instead, they woke up later than they wanted (who could blame them) and didn't realize a thing until they went to the kitchen, turned on the light, or tried to at least. Nothing happened.

Linus went to the living room and tried to turn on a lamp. Nothing there either.

"Power's out," he said, returning to the kitchen.

"What time is it?" asked Ophelia.

Linus shrugged and pointed to the dark face of the digital clock on the counter.

Walter, still in sweats and a T-shirt walked in, looking as if sleep refused to give him up completely. "Hey, mates. Power's out."

Milady walked in. "What a beautiful morning."

"Power's out," said Ophelia.

"What?" She looked around. "I don't understand what you mean."

"The lights don't work," said Walter.

"Oh." She sat down at the kitchen table. "I was thinking I'd better get back in my dress before going back." She shuddered, turning to Linus. "Are you sure ...?"

"I have no idea what to do. I wish I could. But after last night, I'm not taking any chances."

"You did the best you could," Milady said. "Figure it out, but dear heavens, boy, stop feeling sorry for yourself. That's never done anybody any good at any time."

"True," he said.

Ophelia felt a little bold. "Well, the gas stove still works. I'll make us some tea and get out some cookies." She stood on a chair.

Walter looked at her in horror. "You're getting your uncle's shortbread? Ophelia! Why take that kind of chance?"

"Just one. For Milady. She should get to taste them."

Walter didn't mention Milady was from France where they made the best food. Ophelia's heart was in the right place.

She also took down a bag of butter cookies, the kind shaped like a little flower. What a delightful little snack! If some of those don't cheer you up, I've got nothing to offer you. You're on your own.

"That was quite a storm last night, wasn't it?" Milady said.

"What storm?" Ophelia filled the kettle at the sink.

"You didn't hear it?"

The trio all shook their heads.

"No," said Walter.

"It was amazing. Like God and all the angels decided to hold a party," she said.

"How did we miss this?" Walter sat down at the kitchen table.

"It's your youth." Milady smiled. "You all sleep like the dead. Enjoy it while you can."

The sound of footsteps running up the steps alerted them to the doorway. Clarice came rushing through. "I just saw Johann heading into the school with two gas cans!"

Everybody did the math.

"It was him!" Ophelia cried.

"I knew it!" said Walter. "Ophelia, call 9-1-1. Let's go!" *(The lad is a quick study.)*

Everyone else ran down the steps, including Milady.

Ophelia ran to the phone hanging on the kitchen wall, picked up the receiver and put it to her ear. "It's dead." Which also meant all the phones on the street were dead too. She looked around, cursing the fact that none of them had cell phones, not even Clarice, who didn't want one so her parents had to contact her through the school.

She hurried down the steps, hoping against hope that someone, anyone, was home.

By the time the rest of the group made it to the school, Johann had sloshed the fuel around the living room.

"No!" Walter yelled as Madrigal's brother set a match to the fuel.

Johann turned toward the group. "You should never have gotten involved."

"You'll be arrested. You won't get the house," said Clarice as the blaze began to spread up the heavy velvet drapery.

Linus said, "Never mind that!" And he ran back to the kitchen to get water.

"Oh, you're right," said Johann. "But neither will she."

He slipped away through the garden doors.

"The linen closet!" said Walter. "Soak the sheets and towels!"

Clarice ran up the steps behind him, and a minute later they were throwing all manner of linen over the edge of the balcony.

Linus slid into the room with two buckets filled with water. All he could think of was the word *smother*. He dunked the linens into the water and hurried into the living room, trying desperately to stamp out the flames with the sopping fabric.

*Where is the fire department?* he wondered. *Come on!*

Ophelia careened out onto the street like a wolf was at her heels. She ran up to Birdwistell's door. Rapped as hard as she could. He opened it ten seconds later, saw her, and frowned.

"I need to use your phone! Do you have a cell phone?"

"Of course not!"

"What time is it?"

He frowned yet further. "Typical of you to not even know that." He plucked a gold watch from the pocket of his vest. "10:20."

"Thanks!" She ran to the next place. Ronda's hair shop. The pretty lady had already taped a sign to the door.

"Sorry! No power! Closed. Call to Reschedule. We Appreciate Your Patronage."

*Drat!*

Father Lou! Why didn't she think of him sooner?

She ran across the street and down the walk to the back of the manse. "Father Lou!" She beat on the kitchen door with her fists. "Father Lou!"

He opened the door a full fifteen seconds later, fifteen seconds that felt like five minutes. "Oph—"

"Call 9-1-1. Johann set the school on fire!"

"It was him!" Father Lou reached into his pocket for his phone, then punched in the numbers.

*He's so calm! How can he be so calm?*

D'Artagnan entered the kitchen. "Did I hear the school is on fire?"

"Yes!"

"Then let's go see what we can do!"


"Where's the fire department?" Clarice hollered in frustration.

"Where's Madrigal?" Linus asked, flinging a blanket on top of a blazing portion of carpet.

Walter did the same. The heat was almost to the point of unbearable. "She's always gone on Saturday mornings."

Milady ran back and forth from the buckets, dunking towels and bringing them to the other three.

*She could work. She was industrious. Laziness was never the woman's problem. Let's face it, dear ones, it takes a lot of work to be a proper villain.*

She went back to the kitchen to fill the buckets once more.

Clarice wiped a forearm against her forehead. "It's getting dangerous, you guys."

Walter hated to admit it.

Just then Ophelia, D'Artagnan, and Father Lou burst into the room. Flames danced in greater numbers than before.

"We're barely making a dent!" cried Linus.

The smoke began to thicken.

Father Lou looked around. "I'm calling it. Everybody outside!"

"But Madge," shouted Walter as the roar of the fire increased.

"Would rather everybody be alive. Now let's go!" the priest yelled.

They all filed outside to the garden, shutting the door behind them.

Clarice began to cry. Linus put his arm around her shoulder.

Milady became enraged. "Why that ... that pig of a brother of hers!"

"Where's the fire department?" Ophelia cried.

As if on cue, the shrill sound of a siren split the air between the school and the firehouse.

Nobody thought to look at the time.

## twenty-three

# In the Nick of Time Is Much Better Than In the George of Time, Don't Ask Me How I Know That

The blaze took hold just as the fire trucks screeched to a halt on the street. With lightning speed, the firemen hooked up the hoses to the hydrant and pushed their way through the door for the second time in a week. The sitting room would be ruined certainly, but everyone stood there hoping and praying the rest of the building would sustain little damage.

Father Lou shook his head. "This isn't like the other one. He was playing for keeps this time."

"It can't burn down," said Clarice. "Where will I go?"

"I know what you mean," said Walter. He sat down on the grass and stared at the school. "This is horrible."

Ophelia sat next to him and put her arm around him. "It will be all right, Walter. It will work out. Madge will think of something. And if she doesn't, we will. Right?"

"That's right," said Linus, finding that speaking more than a couple of words was actually all right. "We're with you. Rickshaw Street is our home" — he looked at Father Lou — "for all of us."

"And it always will be," said Milady, leaning into d'Artagnan. "No matter where we find ourselves."

"Oui," said d'Artagnan.

Every pair of eyes snapped toward him. He spoke in French!

"The portal!" Ophelia cried. "What time is it?"

"Oh dear." Father Lou looked at his cell phone. "It's 11:07!"

"Four minutes!" Walter cried.

"What are you talking about?" said Clarice.

There was no time to explain. She'd have to know because none of them wanted to hurt Clarice by excluding her. True friends do that sort of thing, you know.

"Let's go!"

Everyone ran toward the bookstore.

Milady followed, tears glistening in her eyes. It was time. Her heart was breaking. How in the world would she survive in the world Dumas created for her? Even if she tried to do the right thing, nobody would believe she was doing it for the right reason.

They entered the room with only two minutes to spare. Father Lou's eyes glistened. "This is the first time I get to see this!"

"What?" asked Clarice.

"Just watch," the priest said. "They'll explain afterward. From what they've told me, this is always the saddest moment of the adventure."

"What—"

"Shhh," he said. "Just watch."

The two stood on the outskirts of the room.

Cato Grubbs stepped out from the corner, and with him

the three musketeers themselves. Porthos, Athos, and Aramis. "Well, well, well!" He held up the brooch with a wicked smile.

Milady, throwing her gown over her Real World clothes, gasped. "Give that to me!"

"No, no, no," Cato replied.

The three musketeers stepped forward, hands automatically reaching for and resting on the hilt of their swords. "Thievery, still, you devil of a woman!" One of the three musketeers said in a deep voice. It was Athos, clearly the leader of the small group, and his eyes were heavily lined, etched with a hardness, and, Ophelia thought, perhaps a hint of sadness.

Tick, tick, tick.

"I need that!" Her eyes flashed like the lightning of the night before.

D'Artagnan eyed her suspiciously, then sadly.

"Don't tell me you've been taken in again by her wily ways," said the broadest of the three, Porthos.

"Ah, young love bites again with its bittersweet sword," replied the third, who had to be Aramis. "I will pray for your deliverance."

*Yes*, Ophelia thought, *definitely Aramis.*

D'Artagnan set his jaw, then he nodded to his similarly clad compatriots.

They drew their swords.

"No!" cried Linus.

"What are you doing?!" shouted Walter. "Put those things away! You'll hurt someone."

Cato nodded. "It's all right, gentleman. I don't think it will come to a swordfight here."

Ophelia ran to Milady's side and took her hand.

"Wait!" D'Artagnan yelled,

"You don't need that, Milady," Ophelia said.

"Yes, I do!" She shook off Ophelia's grasp and threw herself at the mad scientist.

"It's all right, fair maiden," said Porthos. "You are not the first to be taken by Milady's deception."

"No!" Ophelia cried. Had everyone misjudged Milady? Had she really just been pretending to change? Was it all a masquerade? Wait, did Porthos just call her a fair maiden?

Ophelia's heart sank. No, it couldn't be. She loved Milady. They had become each other's friends. How could this be?

Milady tried to reach Cato's now hidden hand. Cato Grubbs laughed a cruel, evil laugh.

"Thirty seconds," said Father Lou, looking at his cell phone.

The struggle continued. Cato laughing, Milady stifling a scream of frustration.

Finally d'Artagnan had enough. He walked over, grabbed Cato's arm and removed the brooch from his hand. "Here!" He handed it angrily to Milady. "We'll deal with this on the other side. Now get into the circle, Madam."

He pulled her inside the white confines of the enchanted circle. "You three as well," D'Artagnan said, his eyes flashing anger. "And thanks for showing up on time."

Fifteen seconds. But the three musketeers didn't move into the circle.

Milday took d'Artagnan's hand, placed the brooch on his palm, and said, "Take this back to the queen. My days of stealing and lying are over."

"Oh, Milady!" Ophelia jumped in and hugged her as the countdown started.

Eleven. Ten. Nine.

"You saved my life, Ophelia, and I will always love you," the Countess de Winter said.

Six. Five.

"I'll always love you too."

Three.

"Get out! Now!" shouted Walter.

Ophelia jumped out. "Good-bye! Good-bye friends."

The pair bowed and held hands as the circle began to glow through the prism.

The rest of the group waved and shouted their regards as the sparks flew from the circle and the smoke began to thicken. The countess's smile was the most beautiful thing any of them had ever seen.

And when the smoke swirled and collected with the great snap, they were left with an empty circle, a hollow sense of loss, and a great relief that two more travelers had made it back safely to their world.

Ophelia opened her mouth to tell her second cousin thrice removed a thing or two. But he'd disappeared as well.

The three musketeers looked at one another, mystified. "What sorcery is this?" Aramis cried. "Get behind me, Satan!"

"No sorcery," Linus said. He sounded a bit deflated as well. "We'll explain everything, but first...wait...look!" Linus hurried over to his worktable. "A note!" He read it aloud.

"Now you've made me really angry, cousins. That brooch would have given me enough money to live on for quite some time. Relatives or not, I will not let you get away with it. What's more, you get a double dose of Dumas. I'm leaving these fellows here with you for the next two days. Have a ball!"

"What in the world is going on?" Clarice looked as if she'd been hit on the head with a big, fat stick of mystery.

"Let's go get hot dogs," said Linus. "And we'll tell you all about it."

Ophelia pointed to Athos, Porthos, and Aramis. "What about these guys?"

"You'll figure it out, sis." He took Clarice's hand and they exited the attic.

Walter grabbed Ophelia's hand in his own. "We'll figure it out together." He looked at the musketeers. "Well, gentlemen, have a seat. We have a lot of explaining to do."

*Great. Just great*, thought Ophelia, until she realized that Walter had yet to disengage his hand from hers. Oh! Well … *Really great!*

*If you, dear reader, want to know what happened to these three, you'll have to get the update in the next book. Tom Sawyer, that young wheeling, dealing upstart will be along for the ride. So there's nothing more to say, really, other than, for heaven's sake go outside! Have a milkshake with your friends! Paint a picture! You can't sit around reading all day, can you?*

# Questions to Ponder

1. The gang was expecting a "good guy" to come through the circle, and Milady showed up instead. Have you ever met someone you thought was a good person and they ended up being hurtful? What happened?

2. Can people really change? Why did Milady come to a different conclusion about how to live her life?

3. D'Artagnan swooped in and saved Milady's life. Can you think of a person who helped you when you couldn't help yourself?

4. The love of money is the root of all evil, the Good Book says. How was this displayed by Johann?

5. Madrigal Pierce is not an easy-going person. What was revealed in the book that shed some light on why she might be this way?

6. Is Cato Grubbs a good guy or a bad guy?

7. Is Linus playing with fire by trying to duplicate Cato's experiments? What would you do?

8. Ophelia is jealous of Milady. Is it because of her beauty, or something else?

9. Who would you bring through the enchanted circle and why?

10. Do you have to do chores like the ones Uncle Augustus assigns the twins?

11. Eleven is a very important number in the Sandwich/ Easterday family. What's your favorite number?

# The Enchanted Attic

## Wrestling with Tom Sawyer

*Author: L.L. Samson*

School is back in session, and all of Kingscross is abuzz with news of a burglar specializing in fine antiques and rare books. Seven Hills Rare Books has battened down the hatches, and meanwhile, preparations are underway for this month's party, "Bare Feet and a Straw Hat Never Hurt Anybody." For the "Evening with Mark Twain," Ophelia is reading Tom Sawyer, and the gang agrees that Tom should be brought into Real World. He'd be a refreshing change, much easier to handle than Captain Ahab and Lady DeWinter, and they could easily pass Tom off as a student. However, once in the attic, Tom immediately picks a fight with Walter, falls in love with Ophelia, and tries to one up Linus's scientific discoveries with tales of treasure hunting and cave exploring. Even more annoying is his propensity to disappear from right under their noses. When the thieving escalates and Ophelia is kidnapped, Tom is determined to save her. After all, he saved Becky Thatcher. The question is, can Tom find Ophelia before the enchanted circle opens for his return to Missouri, or will he fizzle away like the Wicked Witch of the West?

Softcover: 978-0-310-74057-5

*Available in stores and online!*

# Talk It Up!

*Want free books?*
*First looks at the best new fiction?*
*Awesome exclusive merchandise?*

We want to hear from you!

Give us your opinions on titles, covers, and stories.
Join the Z Street Team.